HIND POCKET BOOKS

Teach Yourself

GARDENING

Teach Yourself

GARDENING

PRAMILA MEHRA

HIND POCKET BOOKS
An imprint of Penguin Random House

HIND POCKET BOOKS

USA | Canada | UK | Ireland | Australia
New Zealand | India | South Africa | China | Singapore

Hind Pocket Books is part of the Penguin Random House group of companies whose addresses can be found at www.hindpocketbooks.com

Published by Hind Pocket Books Pvt. Ltd
4th Floor, Capital Tower 1, MG Road,
Gurugram 122 002, Haryana, India

Penguin Random House India

First published in Hind Pocket Books by Penguin Random House India 2019
This edition Published in 2022

10 9 8 7 6 5 4 3 2

The views and opinions expressed in this book are the author's own and the facts are as reported by him which have been verified to the extent possible, and the publishers are not in any way liable for the same.

ISBN 9789353494513

Printed at Repro India Limited

www.penguin.co.in

FSC www.fsc.org MIX Paper from responsible sources FSC® C047271

This is a legitimate digitally printed version of the book and therefore might not have certain extra finishing on the cover.

CONTENTS

CHAPTER 1

Layout of a Garden

The basic layout of a garden depends on the individual's taste. There are no hard and fast rules about the planning of the garden. An amateur gardener may borrow ideas from other gardens. In some gardens paving patterns are pleasing and in others, grouping of plants is pleasing.

Sunlight is also a deciding factor in the basic layout. Some plants thrive in shaded parts of the garden and others need sunlight.

The type of soil in the garden is also one of the deciding factors in planning the basic layout. All types of trees, plants and shrubs cannot be successfully grown in all types of soil.

Armed with all these basic ideas, the gardener should make a plan on paper. A little replanning may be done at the time of planting.

After acquiring the garden measurements, we should plan the permanent main parts, like the herbaceous border, hedges, trees, paths, lawns, orchard and a vegetable plot. Some people may like to put in a small fish-pond or lily-pool. The least productive area should be out of sight of the house and should be used for compost heap, tool-shed and for clothesline, if required. Nursery beds should also be out of sight.

The best view of the garden should be from the drawing-room window and the approach to the vegetable garden should be properly paved. Pergolas and arches add to the beauty of a garden. But such features should not overcrowd any garden.

In large gardens a cut-flower plot may be set aside.

The vegetable garden should preferably be rectangular in shape and surrounded by hedges.

After putting all the surrounding and essential structures like garage, gates, approaches and paths on paper, planting of herbaceous borders, trees and hedges should be planned. The whole garden plot should be divided into different sections.

Types of Soil

The basic layout of a garden, to a large extent, depends on the kind of soil it contains. Although with necessary cultivation, anything can be grown on any type of soil, but it is always better to grow the kind of trees, shrubs, herbaceous plants and vegetables which suit the soil of your garden.

The most fertile soil is the mixture of sand, clay and humus which is very rare to find. Some soils are full of chalk which lack iron and are often sticky. Peas or beans cannot be grown on such soils. Lime-loving flowers like lupins grow best on chalky soil.

Sandy soil contains very little plant food and so needs frequent feeding with fertilizers and manures. Sandy soil is dry and so can be cultivated easily. It is ideal for an early crop.

Peat soils are acidic as they lack lime. This type of soil can be improved with liming. Celery grows well on peaty soils.

Medium loam is the ideal kind of soil containing sand, clay, humus and lime.

Clay soils are one of the best because they contain most of the plant foods. But such a soil is wet and cold and so needs proper drainage. Almost all types of plants thrive in clay soil, provided its texture is improved.

To improve chalky soil, deep digging is required and some of the soil replaced with farmyard manure. This soil requires very little irrigation, otherwise it will become too sticky to work in.

Peaty soil should be limed each year and good drainage is required.

Clay soil requires improvement in texture and proper drainage. Plenty of farmyard manure and little sand should be added. This type of soil should not be given lime at the same time as manure.

Sandy soil needs plenty of manure, leaf-mould, peat and water to make it moisture retaining.

Water-logged soil needs proper drainage which can be provided by digging 2 ft. wide and 3 ft. deep trenches all over the garden plot and filling them with stones, broken bricks, wooden sticks and straw and then filling with top soil.

The whole garden plot needs digging to ensuse free circulation of water and air. Digging exposes the fresh portions of soil to sun, gets rid of weeds and exposes pests to be devoured by birds.

The best way to dig a plot thoroughly is to begin by digging a trench 3 ft. wide and 1 ft. deep. Soil taken out of this trench should fill the last trench on the ground. Then a second trench of the same dimensions is dug and soil from this one is transferred to the first trench. Proceed in this manner until the end of the plot is reached. The last trench is filled with the soil of the first trench.

Farmyard manure can be placed at the bottom of each trench.

For easier digging, the whole plot may be divided in strips 3 ft. wide by making indentations with a spade.

All weeds and turf at the top are buried in the bottom of the trenches, but perennial weeds are removed and burnt.

After digging the garden plot, space should be allotted to the lawn as well as flower beds, in addition to other features of a garden.

Position and size of the bed determines the kinds of plants grown in them. Beds narrower than 4 ft. are not fit for any type of plants except seasonal. Beds for seasonal displays can be rectangular, oval or round.

Borders for herbaceous plants should be wide – about 10 ft. in width – for a good display. They might be curved or irregular in shape in a corner of the lawn.

Trees and shrubs are permanent features of a garden, so should be planted with careful consideration to their ultimate size and size of the garden. Overcrowding the garden with shrubs spoils the neat look and overall effect of any garden. The shrub border should also be at least 10 ft. wide, for proper arrangement of various tall and dwarf varieties.

Hedges are also a permanent feature of a garden and so deserve some careful planning. Two feet of free space is needed on both sides of hedges for their proper growth.

A rose-garden deserves a secluded space allotted to it in big gardens. If possible, it should be surrounded by hedges so that it makes a separate unit.

In a small garden, roses can be planted away from other plants in a group.

Lawns

Lawns kept in good shape add greatly to the beauty of a garden. Velvet-smooth carpet-like lawn needs some extra attention.

Lawns are made by two methods – from seeds or from cuttings.

Preparation of the Site

Grass also needs cultivation and various plant foods and the site needs a thorough preparation.

After clearing the site of all debris, it should be dug at least one foot deep. All perennial weeds are burnt. If the soil is heavy, wood-ash, sand and peat should be dug in to make it porous and light. A sprinkling of bone-meal encourages root growth.

In alkaline soils, plenty of manure, peat and leaf mould should be dug in. Lime and wood-ash should be avoided.

After digging, the soil should be allowed to fallow for a few weeks and then raked to reduce it to even tilth. The ground is then flooded with water and after drying, the surface levelled. Once again the ground is flooded for levelling. After drying, final surface levelling is done. The lawn-level is kept to about two inches below the garden paths.

Lawns from seeds

If a lawn is to be sown with grass seeds, the ground should be divided into 2-yard squares with the help of a garden line and pegs. Sixty to eighty gms. of seeds mixed with sand are enough for this square piece of land. This way an equal distribution of seeds is ascertained. After sowing, a light sprinkling of water is required. When the ground becomes dry, a light roller should be passed over it to settle the seeds.

Thereafter the lawn should be kept moist with a fine spraying of water. Seeds germinate within a month or even earlier.

Heavy seeding keeps the growth of weeds down. When the grass is 2 inches high, it will be ready for its first cutting.

Lawns from Dibbling Grass Roots

For growing grass from cuttings, the same ground preparations are made as for seed sowing. Well developed grass with closed nodes and short textures should be selected. Doob (*Cynodon dactylon*) is the best grass for a lawn. Plant the grass tufts quite deep and about 3 inches apart. After planting (dibbling) is done, pass a light roller over the lawn and sprinkle lightly with water.

After the grass attains a height of 2 inches the first mowing is done keeping the blades one inch above the ground level.

For a finer surface, 1/2 inch thick layer of finely sifted clay and river silt mixed in a proportion of 1:2 should be spread over the lawn after the first cutting.

The lawn should be kept free of weeds. Motha (*Cyperus*) retards the doob growth. As it is very difficult to get rid of it, each growth of motha should be cut below the ground surface so that doob growth can take over.

The best time to prepare a new lawn is either during summers, if free supply of water is available, or during the rains. Growth of grass stops after October.

Although doob grass has a spreading tendency, it grows vertically during rains. After the rainy season all the vertical growth should be checked with close mowing.

Weeding and regular watering is a must.

You should not use the roller too frequently as it checks the growth of grass.

A fertilizer mixture of 10 parts of nitrogen, 6 parts of phosphorus and 4 parts of potassium should be applied in established lawns, 3 to 4 times between March to October.

Annual liming of the lawn is essential. It should be given just before the monsoons. Lime should be made damp before spreading.

In September, an application of ammonia sulphate or nitrate of soda helps the grass to grow. Ammonia sulphate and lime should not be applied at the same time.

Established lawns with hard surface can be revived by raking thoroughly.

Doob grass does not grow well in shade or under the trees, so annual winter grass (*Poa annua*) can be grown there.

For the revival of an established lawn, make a mixture of 2 parts of sulphate of potash, 1 part of ammonia, and 20 parts of sand. Spread about 130 gms. of this mixture per sq. metre, twice, in summer and rainy season.

Dry Wall and Rockery

Dry wall is made with stones or bricks but without cement or mortar. This wall acts as hedge or retaining wall at the end of a terrace or a sunk garden. Whenever a sudden change of level occurs a dry wall is used.

A dry wall with a core of soil in between can accommodate various varieties of rock plants. A double wall is built with about 12 inches of space in between which is packed with soil for planting rock plants.

Before starting to build the dry wall, a soil mixture is made with loam, sand, leaf-mould and garden compost. This soil mixture should be made moist. Plenty of stones, which can be rock stones, sand stones or bricks, are collected. A 12 inches wide and quite deep trench is dug for laying the foundation of the wall. At least two layers of stones should fit into this foundation. The thickest and largest pieces are used for the foundation, then soil and pebbles are rammed in till it becomes level with the ground.

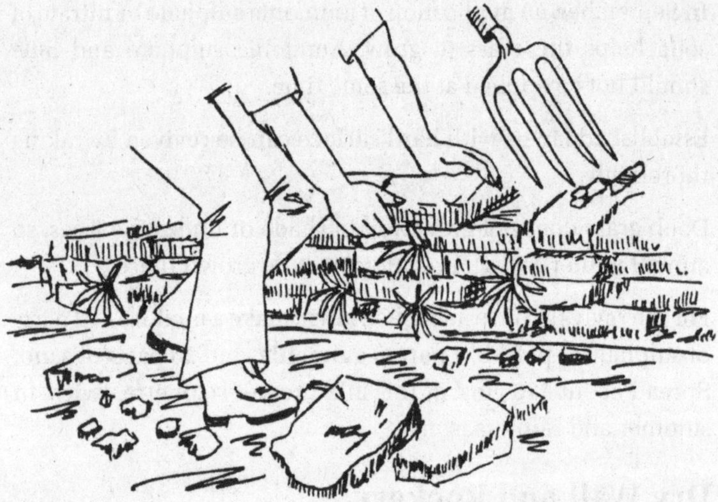

Fig. 1. Plants are put in position as dry wall is being built.

Now the first layer of stones is laid above ground level with the straight edges facing the front. This layer is then covered with about 2 inches of soil. Soil should be rammed firmly in all the crevices and at the back of the stones. Build up the rest of the wall in a similar manner but vertical crevices should not come in a line. Occasionally some space can be left between the stones to make way for plants, but it is much better to plant them while the wall is being made. This way roots will not be damaged. Later on seeds can be sown in soil pockets.

Dry wall looks particularly well in a rockery. It can be of any desired shape but the height should not be more than 4 ft.

Winter is the most suitable time to build the wall and before planting, all the weeds should be pulled out. Spring is the best time for planting. The top of the wall should be covered with thick soil so that the perennials can be planted there.

Ferns and mosses lend an antique look to the dry wall.

Ageratum, verbena, portulaca, *Bellis perennis, Gypsophila elegans, Hymenantherum tenuifolium, B.tripartita* and *Selaginellas* are some of the varieties of plants suitable for the dry wall.

Rockery when properly stocked and planned to look natural and informal becomes a beauty spot of any garden.

Any heap of soil into which rocks or stones are stuck, does not become a rock garden. It can be planned on a raised ground to hide vegetable garden or any unsightly feature behind it.

Some rock gardens are made in shaded spots where annual flowers or grass cannot thrive.

A rockery should have good drainage, so about 2 feet of soil should be excavated from the proposed site and a layer of clinkers and broken bricks should be laid and then filled by fertile and lime-free soil as most of the rock plants do not thrive in lime. Natural stones dug out of hill sides are best for rockeries and all the stones should be buried quite well into the soil. The base for rockery should have some depressions and mounds to lend it a natural look. Stones should be so placed that they have an inward and downward slope. Soil is rammed well between the stones so that plants can root well.

Some rock plants need shade which can be provided by careful placing of a big rock.

Paths in the rock-garden should look natural and informal, so may be laid with stone chippings, grass or stone slabs with small plants growing in between them. In the beginning some established ferns or even annuals growing in pots can be sunk in the rockery. Violets thrive in shaded rockeries. Ferns, palms, crotons, *Asparagus plumosus,* dracaenas and *Ophiopogon intermedius* are some of the shade loving plants.

Amaryllis, freesias, begonias, cinerarias, dianthus and phloxes make a pleasing group.

Seeds and cuttings can make a perfect rockery within a short time. Seedlings should be transplanted very early in life. In autumn, rockeries should be dusted with derris powder to get rid of wood-lice. Weeding should also be done in autumn.

Watering of the rockery should be done very carefully so that the soil does not get washed down.

Annual top dressing of well rotted manure is essential.

Fish and Lily Ponds

Fish or lily ponds add charm even to small gardens. In a big formal garden, a pool may be constructed in the centre of the lawn or in the rock garden.

A small metal wash-tub or even a wooden box can be sunk in the ground to make a small pool. It's rim is camouflaged with rocks, tiles or plants and your pool is ready. If water alone is required a depth of even 12 inches will be enough, but lilies and other floating plants need a depth of 18 inches to 2 feet. Lotus can be planted in one metre depth. If the pool gets full sunlight, fishes can also thrive.

Small pools made with wash-tubs or wooden boxes need a thick coat of non-toxic paints. Slightly bigger pools need proper drainage, thick concrete walls and bottoms, otherwise pools will gradually get empty.

The concrete mixture can be made with one part cement, one part sand, and three part gravel or crushed stone. A final coat of cement may be applied at the top with builder's trowel or with the flat of a spade. The bottom of the pool should be completed first and then the sides are built.

In formal pools, edges can be hidden underneath tiles or slabs. Pools may be lined with a rubber sheet. Several rubber sheets can be welded together, if required. After smoothing the soil at the bottom and sides of the pool, the rubber sheet is pressed down and fitted according to the contours of the pool. Edges are then secured with stones and water is poured in slowly. Edges of the rubber sheets are then trimmed and buried under rocks placed on the rim of the pool. Slabs can be placed over the edges to secure and conceal the rubber sheet. To rid the pool water of certain impurities and to make it fit for fish, add a little phosphoric acid daily till the water is no more alkaline. To test it, dip a pink litmus paper into the water and it should remain pink and not turn blue.

The bottom of the pool is filled with 6 inches of rich loam with 1 inch thick covering of sand. Planting is done directly in this soil and the pool is filled with water only after this planting is done. An alternative method is to fill some wire baskets with soil and lower them into the pool.

Aquatic or oxygenating plants and fish keep the water clean and fresh. Approximately one aquatic per sq. yd. of the water surface, one water lily or lotus for two sq. yds. and one fish for every 30 litres of water should be enough for a pool. Evaporated water should be replaced. Goldfish are ideal for pools as they devour the larvae of mosquitoes and other minute animals.

If a pool is to be kept clear of fish or plants, water can be crystal clear by adding 50 gms. of copper sulphate per 4 kilolitres once a month.

Nymphaea, blue lotus and *nuphar* (lily) are some of the plants recommended for pools. *Salvinia,* azolla, pista and lemna etc., are some of the floating plants.

Sagittaria, typha, hydrilla and *nymphaea* are some of the oxygenators. Lilies should be planted in containers. *Caltha palustris* can be planted along the edges of the pool to conceal them.

CHAPTER 2

Propagation of Plants

Propagation is multiplication or reproduction of plants by sowing, grafting or breeding.

Plants can be propagated in many ways, but two main methods are known as *seminal propagation* – which means raising the plants from seeds – and *vegetative propagation* which means raising and multiplying the plants by stem cuttings, root cuttings, leaf cuttings, and budding and grafting.

Seminal Propagation

Raising the plants from seeds is a comparatively economical method. It is the only way of producing annual and biennials.

Seedlings usually vary from their parent plants, although sometimes the variation is minute. Sometimes seedlings are a distinct improvement on their parent plants. So plant-breeders select the parent plants carefully for obtaining better and new varieties.

If seeds are sown indoors for house-plants, plants from get used to indoor conditions from the very early stage. Seeds differ in size and so need different treatment at the time of storing or sowing them. Smaller seeds have lesser food stored inside them and are, therefore, delicate, needing some extra attention. Seed beds for small seeds should contain very fine tilth so that their delicate seedlings do not perish under lumps.

Some seeds are as big as beans and have hard coats. Such seeds should be soaked for 24 hours in water before sowing.

If sowing is done in a box or pot it should be covered with either glass or polythene sheet and then with brown paper. This way the seeds germinate sooner because the darkness in the seed box causes early root formation. Glass or polythene cover keeps the compost in the seed box moist for a longer time.

When seeds are sown out of doors, seed beds should be prepared with much care. Soil is reduced to a fine tilth and a little sand is added so that soil becomes porous. Seed bed can be dug only when the soil is not too moist. Too much manure is not good for seed beds as then the soil becomes too rich. In such cases seedlings will become too tall and thin instead of sturdy and short.

Seed bed soil can be sieved to make it finer so that tiny seedlings find it easier to come out.

If seeds are sown in boxes or pots, the drainage holes need covering with crocks. Soil inside the seed boxes or pots is made flat so that the upper surface is level and firm.

The best compost for seed beds or seed boxes is two parts of compost manure, one part of sand and one part of leaf mould.

Sowing

Seeds may be sown in drills or sown broadcast and soil should be just moist and not wet and cold. It is better to water the seed bed before fine seeds are sown, to avoid the risk of their floating upto the surface. Sometimes fine seeds are mixed with sand to ensure equal distribution.

Another method to water the seeds sown in pots is to place the pot in a pan of water until the uppermost surface of soil is moist.

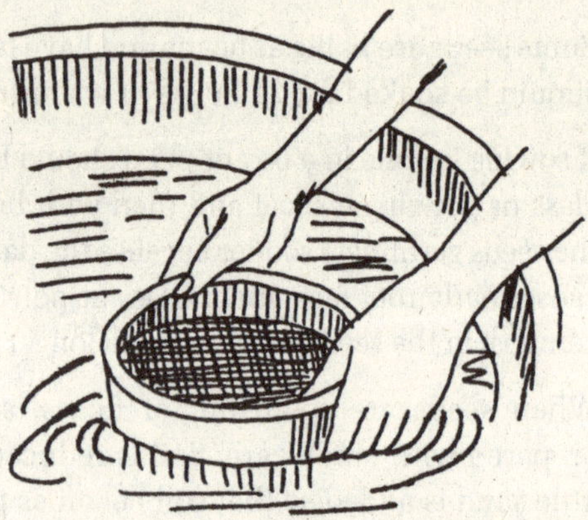

Fig. 2. Watering from below.

If the seeds are sown at the place where they are to germinate, it is better to scatter the seeds irregularly. The seed packet is slit open and seeds are scattered over the well prepared seed bed and covered with soil. The soil may be sifted over the scattered seeds to cover them. The general rule is to cover the seeds with about thrice their own thickness. Very fine seeds may be left uncovered.

Broadcasting in seed sowing is mainly used for annuals sown in seed beds, pots or boxes.

For sowing the seeds in drills, seeds beds are first levelled properly. Then a long stick is pressed into the surface at regular intervals.

Seeds are scattered in these drills and covered lightly with soil. Sowing the seeds in clearly marked lines makes it easier to cultivate the soil in between seeds. Usually, seeds for ornamental plants or vegetables are sown in drills.

Seeds should be sown thinly as plants get more space to grow. Some seeds are grown singly or in pairs like the seeds of sweet peas, beans or corn. If seedlings are overcrowded, they should be thinned out, otherwise the plants will be weak and might decay. Seedlings should be removed for transplanting as soon as they have one pair of true leaves. They are lifted out very carefully with a sharp stick and placed in small holes made with a pointed stick. Soil is then firmly pressed around with fingers. Distance between the seedlings depends on the ultimate size of the plants. At the time of pulling out the seedlings for transplanting, all the roots should be retained.

Soil should also be retained on the roots. This way tiny seedlings adjust in their new beds more happily.

The boxes or flower-beds where the seedlings are to be transplanted should be ready, so that the tiny plants are not exposed to the air for more than a couple of minutes, as exposure at this stage might kill them.

All the seedlings raised under glass for quicker germination are gradually exposed. First they are kept in a sheltered and cool place. Then little by little they are shifted to get more light and air.

Collecting and Storing Seeds

Seeds are alive with their requirement of food stored inside. So seeds should not be kept in airtight containers but in a dry place where they can breathe.

Seeds collected at home should be thoroughly cleaned of all dust before being stored away. Small seeds like poppy seeds can be cleaned of dust and husk by rolling them down a board covered with a rough cloth.

Vegetative Propagation

Vegetative Propagation is multiplication of plants by any method other than from seeds.

Plants are propagated by divisions, cuttings, budding, grafting and layering. Plants produced through vegetative propagation are exact replica of their parent plants, which is not possible by seed propagation. Quick results are possible through this method. But drawback in this method is that plants may carry over the disease from their parent plants.

Propagation by Division

Right after a plant stops flowering it should be lifted out and separated into several plants by dividing the clumps of the roots. Younger and outside portions of the clumps make the best plants as the centre of the clumps is usually half dead. Some clumps are too hard to be separated with hands. In such cases a sharp knife may be used but roots should not be damaged in the process. Each plant which is separated from the main clump should have shoots as well as roots.

Phlox and some forns have hard clumps which are to be broken or cut with a sharp knife. Plants with bulbs, suckers, corms, rhizomers and tubers are propagated by division. Potatoes, lilies, dahlias, violets, tulips are fine examples. Bulbs should not be allowed to grow too close together because then they cannot get enough food.

Most of the plants can be propagated by cuttings. This way existing numbers of plants can be multiplied without extra expenditure. Cuttings can be prepared from roots, leaves or stems. Unlike propagation by division, cuttings are either roots without shoots or leaves without roots. All the cuttings should be taken from healthy plants with a very sharp knife. The length of cuttings depends on the type of plants, trees or shrubs. Selected cuttings from smaller plants should not be longer than 6 inches and cuttings from trees or shrubs can be 8 or 9 inches in length. They vary in length according to the thickness of cuttings. When the cuttings are about 1/4 inch in thickness, only one inch length will be sufficient. The smaller the cuttings are the quicker they grow roots and so chances of survival are more.

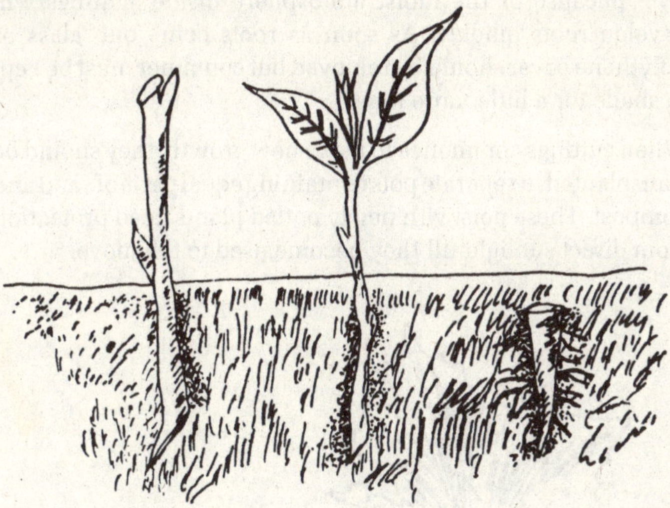

Fig. 3.Cuttings are inserted in sand and root cuttings are buried so that their tops are covered with 1/2 inch soil.

All cuttings are to be kept alive till they develop roots. Best rooting medium is considered to be sand. Cuttings need constant watering in sand and as soon as they develop roots, cuttings should be removed to ordinary compost in a pot as sand does not contain any plant food. For delicate cuttings a mixture of half sand and half leaf mould is best.

When cuttings are planted in boxes or pots, the drainage should be good, with a thick layer of crocks at the bottom. In pots, the cuttings are planted close to the rim and then centre of the pot is watered. The correct way to plant cuttings is to make a hole in the soil and at least one third of the length of cutting is buried in it. Soil is then firmly pressed around. The bottom of the cutting should firmly touch the base of the hole.

Newly planted cuttings cannot tolerate direct sunlight, so the pot or box containing them should be kept in shadow. Cuttings may be covered with glass or polythene to minimize evaporation. Because of the moist atmosphere inside, cuttings will develop roots quickly. As soon as roots come out, glass or polythene cover should be removed but container must be kept in shade for a little more time.

When cuttings commence to make new growth, they should be transplanted in separate pots containing equal parts of sand and compost. These pots with newly potted plants need protection from direct sunlight till they become used to the move.

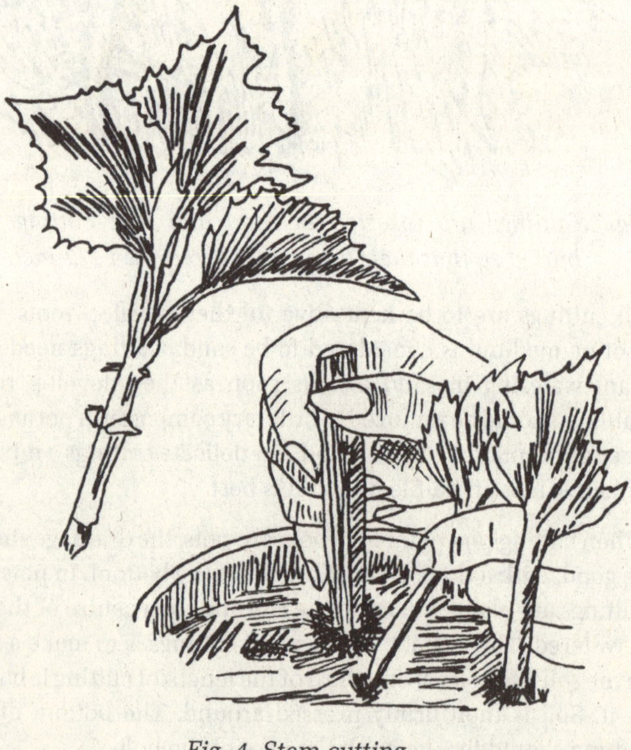

Fig. 4. Stem cutting.

Cuttings root more rapidly if sprinkled with lukewarm water for a few days.

If cuttings are planted outside in garden beds they need protection from sun and hot winds. A shelter can be built out of gunny bags or straw.

The best time to take cuttings is during the dormant period of plants. Cuttings from the tropical shrubs and trees should be taken just before rainy season.

Cuttings from soft wood strike roots earlier than the cuttings from the woody trees. All cuttings grow well if parent plants are vigorous and healthy.

For very delicate cuttings a pot containing half sand and half compost should be used.

Softwood cuttings are ready in about one month for transplanting.

Stem cuttings vary in length according to their thickness.

Fig. 5. Heel.

When the cuttings are made from young, soft shoots, they are known as *soft wood cuttings*. Chrysanthemums and carnations are fine examples. Such cuttings are usually from 2 to 4 inches in length and are cut off just below a joint or a node with a very sharp knife. Lower leaves are then carefully removed and cutting is ready for planting (Fig. 4).

Some cuttings prove to be more successful if severed halfway between nodes like the cutting of a clement plant.

Hard Wood Cutting

They are taken from trees or shrubs

during their dormant period or when they are shedding. Young shoots are pulled in downward motion so that a strip of old wood is retained on the cuttings. This 'heel' or 'tongue' is neatly trimmed with a sharp knife before insertion.

Roots are formed on this larger surface provided by 'heel'. These cuttings should be inserted in pots, boxes or garden beds in the manner described earlier. Hard wood cuttings are usually 9 to 15 inches in length. Rose species are fine examples.

It helps if hard wood cuttings are prepared from firm, young wood formed during the previous year.

Root Cuttings

Plants with fleshy roots such as gaillardias, hollyhock or phlox can be propagated by root cuttings. When parent plants are in dormant stage, they can be lifted out. Reasonably thick roots are then detached and cut into 1 to 2 inches long pieces. Tops of the cuttings are cut level and base on a slant so that it is easier to distinguish the top from the base. These root cuttings are then fully buried in sandy soil.

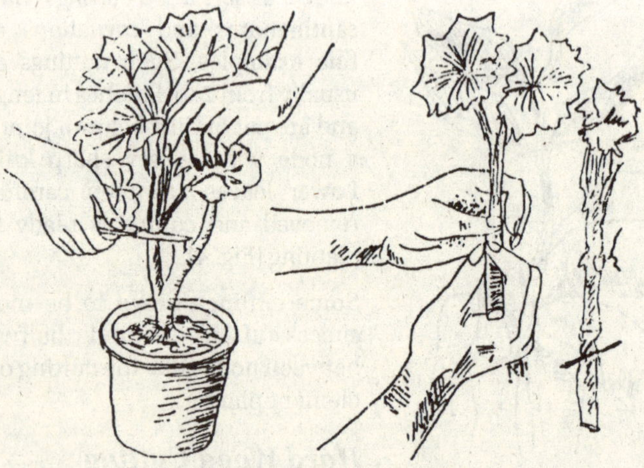

Fig. 6. Preparing a root cutting.

These root cuttings need the same treatment as soft wood cuttings.

Leaf Cuttings

Leaf cuttings are taken during autumn or winter. Fully grown leaf is cut with a dormant bud at its base and a little of stem attached to it. This leaf cutting is then inserted in sand and leaf mould mixture and kept covered with glass, till roots and tiny plantlets are formed. Violets can be propagated by leaf cutting. Sometimes the veins of the leaves are cut in such a manner that the cuts do not reach the other side. Then leaves with their cut side downwards are laid flat in the propagating box filled with sand and pegged down with a piece of wire. Begonias can be propagated by such methods.

Cuttings Prepared in Water

Some cuttings develop roots in water in a shorter time. Ivies are an example.

The vase of glass used for the purpose should be opaque and only one or two inches of bottom should be immersed in water. The portion which is inside the water must contain at least one bud. Vase may be filled with sand sodden with water, and cuttings inserted into it. When cuttings develop tiny roots, they should be potted in compost for a short period and then transferred to the desired place.

Layering

Propagation of plants is done through layering also, which means shoot of a plant is fastened down in soil to take roots. Before burying any part of the stem an upward cut is made through a node. The shoot should not be entirely severed. This incision can be about 1 to 3 inches long and is made in such a way that a 'tongue' is formed. This 'tongue' should be kept open while insertion in soil is made.

Incision in stem helps in checking the flow of sap and forces the formation of roots.

The bent down stems are kept buried in soil with the help of a bent wire or weighed down with a stone. A climbing rose can be propagated by layering. Such plants retain all the characteristics of the parent plants. Soil in which injured shoots are buried for layering should be sandy. Sometimes small pots containing sand and compost are plunged deep near the parent plant for layering. Then young shoots are half severed and pegged into these pots.

Sometimes a stem cannot be bent enough to reach ground level. In such cases, air layering is needed. Stem is cut half way and then wrapped around thickly with moss. It is then covered with polythene to keep the moss damp.

Fig. 7. Layering.

After some time roots will grow. When there are plenty of them, the layer can be severed completely and potted separately. Carnations, roses and most of the shrubs can be propagated by layering. Soft wood plants take about six weeks to root but hard wood plants may take upto a year.

Some plants such as violets or strawberries form runners which eventually root from the underside of the stem. These roots grow around the node. It will help runners to root properly if stem near the node is pegged down with a bent pin or a brick.

Grafting and Budding

Grafting Propagating the plants by grafting means that scion of the plant, from which propagation is desired, is joined to the stem of an allied plant known as stock. Grafting is done during the plant's dormant period. Roses and fruit trees are mostly propagated by grafting.

When scion is much smaller than stock in diameter, rind or crown grafting is needed. A 3 to 4 inches long piece of young firm shoot is taken from the plant to be propagated. A wedge-like cut is made at its lower end. The top of the stock is cut cleanly across. Then straight incision is made in the bark of the stock and forced open with a sharp knife. Wedged end of the scion is then inserted inside the bark of the stock and pushed down. To hold the stock and scion firmly together they are bound tightly with a raffia and then covered with polythene to exclude the air.

When scion and stock are similar in diameter, 'whip' or 'tongue' grafting is done.

A wedge-like cut is made in scion and then a reverse slit is made from the bottom of the wedge to form a 'tongue'. Similar slits are made in stock also but in reverse so that 'tongues' of both scion and stock coincide with each other and fit snugly. They are then bound tightly with raffia and covered with polythene.

In all forms of grafting, stock must not be allowed to make any growth. Growth from scion starts within a few weeks.

In grafting the new growth will inherit all the qualities from scion but actual size of the new plant might be influenced by the stock.

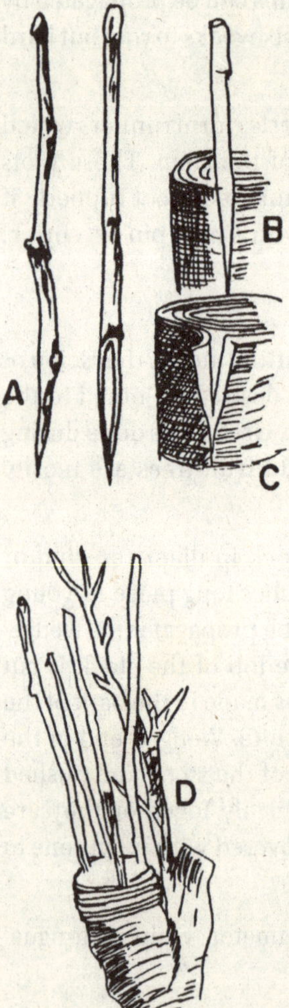

Fig. 8.A - Rind grafting is done when stock is thicker than scion.

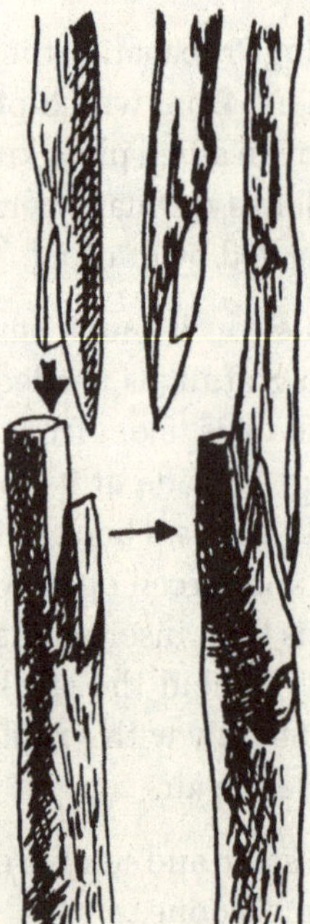

Fig. 8.B - Whip grafting is done when stock and scion are same in thickness.

Budding for propagation is done during the parent plant's growing season. Scion consists of growth buds which are taken from 6 to 10 inches long ripe shoots. A bud with its leaf stalk intact should be removed from the stem with a very sharp knife. A cut should be started from about an inch away from the bud and carried through the wood behind the growth bud and carried upto an inch above the bud. Now sever this shield-like portion and remove the wood from it.

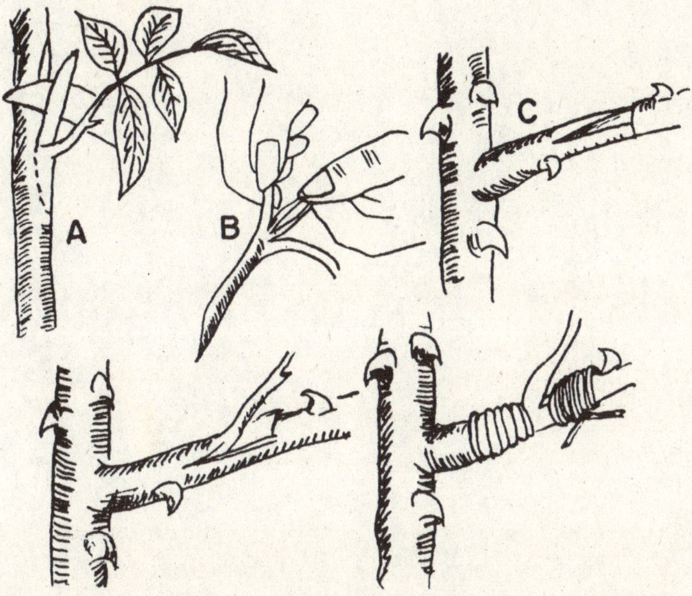

Fig. 9. A Growih bud is removed with a sharp knife.
B Removal of wood from behind the bud.
C T-cut is made in the stock.
D Bud is inserted and tied.

Stock is prepared by making a T-like incision on at least a year old shoot. This incision is then opened with a sharp knife. The shield-like bud portion is then inserted inside and bound firmly with raffia or string. No growth should be allowed on stock.

CHAPTER 3

Manures and Fertilizers

Manure is an essential plant food which contains a large amount of humus. Plants take their food from the soil and must be replaced. Manure provides three main plant foods, namely, nitrogen, potash and phosphate. Farmyard manure is the dung of horses, cows, sheep or poultry and it contains all the essential plant foods.

Manures

Nitrogen helps in the growth of leaves and stems.

Potash encourages healthy growth, good flavour and colour of flowers and fruits.

Phosphate promotes the growth of fruits, flowers and roots. Poultry manure is considered to be best of all farmyard manures. Bonemeal is very slow acting and so is effective for a longer period. It is ideal for roses and fruits. 60 to 70 grams of bonemeal is enough for 1 square metre of land.

Woodash is a good source of potash and should be raked into the top soil. It helps root crops to grow well.

Animal Blood, if used in small quantities for potted plants, makes them grow rapidly. It contains a large percentage of nitrogen.

Lime adds calcium to the soil but in excess destroys humus and nitrogen and sometimes plant foliage turns yellow. Lime should not be applied deeper than 3 or 4 inches and must not be used at the same time as sulphate of ammonia.

Liquid Manure is prepared either with cowdung mixed with water and left to rot, or with any soluble chemical fertilizer. It is a quick acting stimulator for the plant.

All manures such as dung, leaf mould and compost are organic.

Fertilizers

Fertilizers are concentrated forms of inorganic plant foods. These are nitrogenous fertilizers containing nitrate of soda and sulphate of ammonia. They are very strong and quick acting. Sulphate of ammonia is good for grass.

Phosphatic Fertilizers are in the form of superphosphate of lime and bonemeal. They are good for fruits, flowers and roots.

Diseases and Pests of Plants

Any garden, be it small or big, is sometimes attacked by some diseases or pests. It is impossible to exclude them from any garden but they can be checked and kept under reasonable limits.

Amateurs should be able to make rough diagnosis of various diseases and pests, and thus provide treatment. This chapter will help the reader to recognize some common garden diseases and pests.

Diseases

Damping Off

Seedlings in nursery beds are affected by this disease and they collapse because of infection caused by fungi in the soil.

Damping off destroys roots or stems near soil level. Sometimes when seedlings topple off at soil level, beginners might think that some pests have bitten them off, but the stems destroyed by the damping off are blackened, whereas pests do a clean job of it. Sometimes overcrowding of seedlings causes the spread of this disease and occasionally it is started through the infected seeds.

Soil in nursery beds should not be kept too wet and cowdung must never be used there. Seeds can be treated with fungicide which contains cuprosan, cuprous oxide and fytolan. 2 grams of fungicide is sufficient for 1 kilogram of seeds.

The soil of a nursery or seed-boxes should be sterilized with formalin.

Powdery and Downy Mildews

White, powdery growth on leaves and stems is caused by powdery mildew. Plants look as if they are dusted with white powder. Roses, daisies, peas and apples are some of the plants which are usually affected by this disease. Leaves turn yellow in patches and shed early. Stems are also spotted sometimes. Affected plants should be dusted with sulphur powder. Karathene WD also cures powdery mildew.

Downy mildew is less distinctive because white mould is fainter and spreads on the undersides of the leaves which eventually develop yellow spots or turn yellow and shed early. Spray with a Bordeaux mixture.

Treatment in both the diseases should be started early.

Rusts

Rust disease causes rust-coloured spots on the leaves and sometimes on the stems also. These spots are in various shapes and sizes and cause decay. Fungicidal sprays help. Hollyhocks and antirrhinums are badly affected by rust-spots. It is difficult to cure rust so it is better to destroy the plants – if only a few are affected, otherwise the leaves should be burnt and the plants should be frequently sprayed with Bordeaux mixture.

Black Spot

It affects roses and produces round black spots on rose leaves, which fall off early. After sometime, the rose bush becomes a skeleton. All prunings and fallen leaves should be burnt. This disease also affects fruits, including pears and apples. Frequent spraying with Captan helps.

Blight

Blight produces black spots and yellow patches on the leaves. Slowly, leaves lose their green colour and become yellow. Infected leaves have a white growth around brown or black spots on their undersides.

Potato blight produces dark spots on the leaves. A white fungi growth is there around these spots, which contains spores of fungus. When these spores (seeds) fall on other leaves they spread the infection. Wind also spreads infection to other plants. When these spores are washed down to the tubers, they also become infected. Potatoes develop brown patches of decay. Tomatoes are affected by the same disease. Spray with Bordeaux mixture is the best remedy. Seeds should be brought from reliable nurseries to ensure that they are disease-free.

Anthracnose

This disease produces dark spots on leaves as well as on fruits. A pink fluid oozes out of these spots and finally leaves shrivel up and die. Fruits become insipid. Fruits are treated with Captan and plants sprayed with Bordeaux mixture.

Viruses

Viruses cause various kinds of diseases which are difficult to diagnose with accuracy. Sometimes, leaves get deformed or spotted and twisted or narrow. There is no effective cure for virus diseases, so all infected plants must be destroyed

Botrytis

Botrytis is a fungus disease and attacks various plants causing softness, decay and blackening. A grey, fluffy mould appears later on. Tomatoes, vines, lettuces, geraniums, strawberries, cucumbers and melons are mostly affected by this disease. Beans get chocolate spots due to this disease.

Damp conditions should be avoided and plants should be dusted with flowers of sulphur.

White Rot

White rot usually attacks onions when they are grown in the same plot for a number of years. When this disease attacks onions the bulbs can be pulled out very easily because they do not develop any roots. Leaves droop and turn yellow.

The whole crop should be burnt and onions must not be grown in the same spot for many years.

Pests

Aphids

Aphids are plant lice known as green flies, black flies, etc. They are small, soft creatures mostly without wings and cluster around tips of young shoots and on the undersides of leaves to suck the sap. Aphids check the growth of the plant and deform it and also carry the disease from one plant to another. They lay eggs on the tips of young shoots of fruit trees, which should be destroyed.

Spraying with nicotine or pyrethrum is effective.

Some aphids attack the roots of the plants. Such plants are lifted out and dipped in a solution of pyrethrum. Some of the solution should be poured into the holes from which the plants have been removed. Pyrethrum is not harmful for human beings, so fruits and vegetables from the plants sprayed with pyrethrum can be eaten after a week or so. Green flies usually attack roses, lettuce, green peas and flowering plants. Grey flies attack pears and apples and black flies attack beans, chrysanthemums and ferns.

Woolly Aphids

Woolly aphids produce a cotton-like white substance on the bark and the root of fruit trees, especially apple trees, causing premature fall of fruit and leaves.

Ants

Ants harm plants by loosening the soil around them, especially in pots and boxes. Ants may carry aphids from one plant to another. They sometimes harm fruits and blossoms also.

Weevil

Weevil is a quarter of an inch long, grey haired insect with markings on its wings in yellow. This insect bores holes in the flowers with its snout and lays eggs there. It feeds on leaves and makes circular holes on the margin of the leaves. Weevil is almost invisible if it falls on the ground.

Seedlings of peas and beans are usually attacked by it. Spraying or dusting with DDT is effective.

Caterpillar

Caterpillars are larvae of moths and butterflies and have short legs and distinguishable heads. They do not suck sap but feed on leaves, fruits and flowers. Caterpillars particularly harm the cabbage crop. Spraying with nicotine, derris or pyrethrum before harvest time is effective.

Capid Bugs

There are various species of capid bugs which suck the sap and cause leaves and fruits to get deformed. Spraying and dusting with nicotine or DDT is effective. In hills, spraying should be done in winter.

Carrot Fly

Carrot fly is a quarter of an inch long, greenish black fly which lays its eggs below the soil surface. When carrot plants are thinned, soil around them should be made firm so that egg laying becomes difficult. This pest feeds on carrots and causes the leaves to wilt and become reddish.

The plot for sowing carrots should be changed every year.

Onion Fly

Onion fly looks like grey house-fly and lays its eggs on onion's neck or in the soil nearby. Soot spread along rows of onions deters it.

Gall Fly

The gall fly is of a bright, metallic colour and deforms twig ends and leaves of ornamental trees.

Spraying with nicotine and derris helps in getting rid of this insect.

Saw Fly

Saw flies attack fruits and damage apples, plums, etc. It produces a white maggot which spreads upto the centre of the fruits, causing their premature fall.

Some of these flies eat surface of leaves, making them transparent. Dusting with derris is effective.

Leaf Miners

Leaf miners tunnel into leaves, so insecticides do not easily harm them.

Spraying with nicotine helps in cases of severe attacks.

Slugs and Snails

Slugs and snails attack during wet weather. They usually eat leaves and young shoots at night. Insecticides do not harm them. Garden lime deters them. Spraying with metaldehyde is effective but must be repeated frequently.

Harmful Birds

Some birds do much damage in the garden. Soft fruit should be covered with mesh netting. Scarecrows scare away some birds.

Garden Friends

Earthworms are garden friends as they make the soil fertile and drainage is also improved because they break the soil into fine particles.

Owls are also garden friends as they eat mice, rats, beetles, etc., which are garden foes.

Canker

Once it attacks apples, canker, is very difficult to cure. Rose canker also causes a lot of trouble. Fungus eats into the wood, especially the older branches or the main trunk and causes deep wounds. Eventually, the flow of sap is checked and the whole tree dies.

Affected branches should be burnt. Drainage should be improved. Heavy sub-soil should also be avoided.

There are many pests found in the garden but only the main ones are mentioned here which are likely to confront an average gardener.

CHAPTER 4

House-Plants

Indoor gardening helps to brighten and soften the interiors of our homes. Flowering and foliage pots bring with them some of the beauty and warmth of nature.

Selecting the plants for interiors requires some planning. Climate, space and placing of pots are the main points to consider before selecting the house-plants. These are the basic needs of healthy plants.

The plants best suited to your kind of climate will grow more easily. Overcrowding of plants mars their beauty and lends a cluttered and untidy look to your home. So placing of pots should be such as to show them off to their greatest advantage. Their shape and texture should supplement the furnishings in your home interiors. Some plants, like rubber plant – *Ficus elastica* and *Monstera deliciosa* look ideal against a plain wall.

Some climbing plants, with little training, can be converted into screens or room dividers, or as cover for an untidy part of a wall.

All plants need fresh air and light but a few can flourish even in dark surroundings. Usually, the plants with dark, glossy and thick leaves need less light, and can survive even in dark corners of the house. *Monstera deliciosa* and *Ficus elastica* are fine examples.

Crotons, coleus and all varieties of ferns and palms are suitable for both indoor and outdoor potting. But if these plants are kept outdoors, they cannot stand direct sunlight.

Some seasonal flowers can be grown in pots and then kept indoors. Chrysanthemums, carnations and many annuals thrive in pots and are ideal for pot growing even for flower shows.

A few thumb varieties of roses can be grown in pots. At the time of buying pot plants, you should have a definite idea in your mind about the kind of plant you want and its place outside or inside your house.

Seeds and plants should never be bought from door-to-door salesmen. Plant nurseries are more reliable.

Always select a healthy plant, which should have a crisp, clear and perfectly undamaged foliage. Stems should be firm and the plant should have a healthy look.

Check plants for any evidence of pests. Undersides of leaves and joints on the main stem should be particularly checked. In an infected plant, scale insects stick very close to stems or leaves and unless seen very minutely, look like part of the plant. Some plants are infected with red spider which is a tiny mite collected underneath the leaves in large numbers under a cobweb. This can be detected with a magnifying glass only.

It is better to buy small but well-grown young plants. They adjust more easily to their new surroundings. But if you want to buy a large plant, see that it is well staked and no damage has been done to the stem by an over-tight string.

At the time of buying flowering plants, check that they have strong healthy buds in plenty.

Plants showing roots at the top or at drainage holes should never be bought as they need immediate repotting.

For pots, it is always good to buy seeds from reliable nurseries.

This way your plants will adjust to their surroundings from the very beginning.

A choice of flowering plants for pots is given below. The kind of individual care they need is discussed in a separate chapter.

Salvia, petunia, cosmea, portulaca and marigold can be grown in pots quite successfully and most of them will be flowering till the time of winter sowing.

Flowering Annuals for Monsoons

These should be sown by the end of May or early June :

Balsam, cockscomb (*Celosia plumosa*), marigold and zinnia.

Winter Flowering Annuals for Pots

These should be sown in September or October:

Amaryllis, antirrhinum, aster, azalea, begonia, calendula, carnation, cineraria, daisy, dianthus, gerbera, hollyhock, hydrangea, larkspur, nasturtium, pansy, petunia, phlox, stock and verbena.

Hanging Plants

Asparagus, *Campanula,* ferns, *Jasminum, Selaginella,* tradescantia.

Pot-Plants for Foliage

Asparagus, aspidistra (palm), *Begonia rex*, Calamondin (*Citrus mitis*), codiaeum (croton), coleus, eucalyptus, ferns, rubber plant (*Ficus elastica*), *Kochia*, arrowroot plant (*Maranta arundinacea*), *Manetti*, monstera, sansevieria, tradescantia, zebrina.

Potted Flowering Plants from Bulbs

Allium ursinum, crocus, daffodil, hyacinth, narcissus, *Scilla*, tulip.

Climbers in Pots

Bougainvillea, *Clitoria*, *Clematis flammula*, honeysuckle (*Lonicera periclymenum*), *Pergularia, Sligmaphyllums*, etc.

Pots and Manure

Pots

They are available in all kinds of materials, shapes and sizes but the most common ones are made of porous, baked clay. Nearly all pots have a drainage hole at the base and a thicker rim at the top.

Red-clay pots are the most popular and are also inexpensive. Their porous surface makes it possible for plants to soak or release moisture. But these pots should be soaked and washed thoroughly before use. All previously used pots should also be cleaned properly before use again.

Use 3-inch pots for seedlings and about 8-inch pots for decorative plants. Pots larger than these are harmful as pot soil unoccupied by roots may become sour. So at the time of repotting, plants should not be shifted to more than 2-inch larger pots. Many plants do not flourish unless their roots are pot bound, but usually when roots come upto the surface or reach drainage hole, plants are ready for repotting.

Some people prefer plastic pots for their more decorative value. As they are not so porous, plants in such containers need very little water. A plant in a clay pot which needs water nearly once a day, needs it only once in 3 or 4 days when potted in a plastic container. So one may over-water a plant in a plastic pot and harm it.

Glazed pots are also more decorative than clay ones. Water does not evaporate easily from such pots, so moisture is retained for a larger time. Such pots are good for the indoors.

But whatever kind of pots you possess, your plants need constant care and only then they can survive and thrive.

Manure

The best soil for all kinds of pot plants, except cacti, is two parts garden soil, one part leaf-mould and half the quantity of coarse sand, to make the mixture porous. To this mixture, add a handful of ground lime-stone and crushed charcoal for each pot.

Animal manure should be added later as top dressing when the plant is well established.

Preparing the Pots

All the used pots need thorough cleaning. For 3-inch pots, one piece of crock to cover the drainage hole is enough but for bigger pots, a layer of crocks is essential for better drainage. Nearly one-fourth of the pot should be laid with crocks and pebbles at the bottom. If a pot does not have any drainage holes, about one-third of the pot should be filled with crocks and pebbles. Then cover this drainage layer with a piece of sacking or coconut fibres so that the soil is not washed down and roots can have as much air as they need. Now potting soil is added. After a thin layer of soil, place the plant in position, spreading its roots in the soil. Then more soil is pressed around the plant so that no air pocket is left around the roots. Potting soil should come up to 1 inch below the rim. Now, water the plant. If all the water is absorbed, more soil should be pressed in and if the water stays at the surface, the soil should be made more loose.

At the time of repotting, knock the plant out of the pot by holding it upside down. Then place the plant in a well prepared 2-inch larger pot and fill in the additional soil all around it. Hanging baskets should be first lined with moss and then filled up with potting soil.

Potting Soil for Cacti

Cacti need a more porous compost. One part of garden soil, one part of coarse sand, one part of small pieces of broken flower pot and a handful of charcoal and eggshells for each pot is considered to be a successful potting soil for cacti.

Care for Potted Plants

Healthy potted plants are ensured if proper and timely care is taken of them.

All indoor plants must get the right amount of air, light, moisture, correct feeding and proper and regular care. If you keep a few potted plants inside your house for decorative value, they must get enough fresh air, and they should be kept out during the night. Indoor plants must have a certain amount of sunlight. Plant leaves manufacture the carbon they need by taking in energy from sunlight. When direct sunlight does not reach them, plants are satisfied with reflected light. But light they must have. A few plants can survive in dark corners of the house also. Monstera and cacti are fine examples.

Watering the plants at the proper time is essential for their growth. Too much watering is the single main cause of death of indoor plants, especially during winter. Overwatering drives out the air from the pots and plants die or suffer due to lack of air.

Leaves of the plants should be kept clean and washed regularly with water so that they can breathe.

During summer, the outdoor potted plants need watering twice a day and house-plants need watering only once a day. During winter, plants need very little watering. Foliage plants have their dormant period during winter, so they need less water.

Watering should be done in the evening or early morning. To check if the plant needs water, the pot should be tapped with a thick wooden stick. If a hollow sound is heard, it shows that the plant needs water, otherwise a dull sound will be heard.

When plants are in their growing stage, they need more water. Plants with thick, shiny and hairy leaves need less water. Potted plants are always fed by liquid manures. Even animal manure should be given in liquid form.

The amount of feeding a plant needs depends on its size. But normally a potted plant needs feeding once a fortnight. Repotted or newly-potted plants do not need any feeding for a couple of months.

A flagging and drooping plant should not be fed.

A completely dry soil also does not accept extra feeding because root-hair get scorched.

Plants should be fed in the evening so that they can absorb slowly.

Plants need a tiny dose of manure; an overdose might prove to be harmful.

A few year old foliage plant can be helped by removing its top soil and replacing it with fresh soil. Roots should not be disturbed.

Pot-plants should be staked properly so that stems can have some extra support.

Climbers need a more elaborate staking. A trellis-work made of split bamboo serves the purpose excellently. Staking and tying of plants should be as inconspicuous as possible, so stakes can be painted green. A constant watch and timely care ensures happy pot plants. All dead and yellowing leaves should be removed and dead flowers cut off.

Broken stems should be pruned with a sharp knife.

Surface soil needs loosening when dry, so that roots can breathe more easily.

Stems and leaves should be inspected regularly for any sign of disease.

Leaves should be washed or wiped clean so that they can breathe freely.

Pots should be kept clean. Mossy growth on the outer side of clay pots makes them less porous.

Rain water is very nourishing.

Care of the Plants during Holidays

Whenever all the family members go for a holiday together, the care of plants is a problem. Outdoor plants in garden beds or pots can be looked after by the gardener, but house-plants cannot be left out in the open for long, especially during summer.

The best solution to the problem is to leave them with some nursery man. If you leave them with your friends, leave instructions that they are not to be over-watered.

Cacti and succulents hardly pose any problem. You may give them a thorough watering and leave the pots in the centre of the room so that hot sunshine cannot reach them. Cacti can survive for nearly 3 weeks like this without any further care.

If there is a danger of your plants dying of lack of moisture, fill some buckets and, if possible, your bathtub with moistened peat. Put the pot plants inside and see that pots are fully surrounded by peat. This way, there will be less chances of evaporation.

Climbing plants, which cannot be shifted without any damage can be protected with a screen to provide shade and prevent evaporation.

People not living on ground floors may leave their plants on the shaded balcony at the back of the house. This way plants may have their full share of air and light as well.

If there is a shaded place in your garden, you may bury pots up to the rims in the soil. This way, they can survive for a little time without water.

Check your plants thoroughly for any sign of disease and pests.

Trim off all the buds before leaving, so that your plants bloom later on when you are back.

Bulbs and Corms in Pots

Flowering bulbs and corms can be grown in pots and even in bowls quite successfully.

Well developed bulbs should be planted in ordinary pots. If these pots have drainage holes, ordinary light garden soil without manure should be used. Some charcoal must be mixed in the bowl-soil to keep it sweet.

Bulbs are planted in pots or bowls in such a way that they are not overcrowded, but they can be planted fairly close to each other and then buried to a depth of about 4 inches in sand, ash or peat. The bowls or pots containing the bulbs, should be kept in a dark place – under the beds or in dark cupboards and watered frequently. After 8 or 9 weeks, when the bulbs begin to grow, pots can be brought out for display in the house.

Different types of bulbs should not be mixed in one pot or bowl, as their height and flowering times might differ.

Some people store the bulbs outdoors under 3 or 4 inches of sand or peat or ash, and when they start growing, transplant them in pots or bowls and shift them indoors. Bulbs are grown in boxes also and when ready and well developed they can be transferred to bowls.

Hyacinths can be grown in water also. The bulbs are set on a sand bed in a bowl or glass containing a little water and their roots will begin to grow. Water is kept sweet with a few pieces of charcoal. A little water is added from time to time. These bulbs are also in the dark for about 8 weeks. By then the bulbs start growing roots.

When bulbs stop flowering, their foliage should be allowed to die down in its own time. Then they should be dug out carefully with roots intact and stored either outdoors in partial shade or in boxes.

Some of the bulbous plants flower during summer, which should be sown in the beginning of May and are grown quite successfully in pots and bowls. *Hymenocalis*, *Speciosa*, narcissus, *Sprekelia formosissima*, *Nerine flexuosa*, *Dianella intermedia*, *Amaryllis belladonna* and begonia are some of the summer flowering bulbous plants.

Dahlia, canna and *Nymphaea* are winter flowering bulbous plants. *Amaryllis belladonna*, narcissus, dahlia, *Dicaryum pendulam*, agapanthus Africans, etc., are spring flowering bulbous plants.

Alpinia sanderae, water lilies, caladium and alocasia, etc., are such bulbous plants which flower during the rainy season. Crocus, daffodil, hyacinth, iris, narcissus, tulip, snowdrop, *Scilla*, lily of the valley and muscari are some of the more ornamental bulbous plants suitable for pots.

CHAPTER 5

Perennials

Perennials are those plants which last for years and so lend permanence to any garden.

Some perennials flower and some do not. Herbaceous perennials have a soft growth and flower for a long time. Thereafter, most of them die down to ground level and grow again in spring.

Woody perennials are trees and shrubs which possess a hard wood framework. Most of the shrubs and trees are evergreens, so they lend permanent charm to a garden all the year round. A permanent herbaceous border is an essential feature of a large garden but in a small garden, this is not practical.

Some of the freely flowering perennials can be grouped together to make a pretty display throughout the year. Lily, chrysanthemum, gaillardia and iris are fine examples. These plants are not renewed each year and, given care, they may last for years.

Some of the herbaceous perennials are excellent as cut-flowers. *Limonium bonduellii* bears tubular pink and white flowers and has a nice fragrance. *Limonium latifolium*, *Lupinus polyphyllus*, *Myosotis sylvatica* and *Felicia bergeriana* are some of the flower bearing perennials.

Planting of perennials for a pleasing effect requires some

planning. Planted in irregular groups with taller varieties at the back and smaller ones in front looks quite effective.

Preparation of Soil and Planting of Perennials

Soil preparation for perennials should be thorough, as once planted, they are not disturbed for many years. The soil should be fairly rich with a good drainage, although many perennials bloom even in dry or poorly drained soils. Some perennials flourish even in wet soil and in the shade.

The trench for perennials is dug deep. The bottom of the trench is then filled with well rotted compost as fresh manure harms roots of herbaceous plants.

All perennial weeds should be removed thoroughly at the time of digging. The ground for perennials needs at least two diggings. If the ground becomes too wet because of rains, planting of herbaceous perennials should be delayed.

Planting of perennials can be done either when they have just started to grow or when they have stopped growing in winters.

Holes for perennials are dug deep enough for the roots to spread fully according to their natural growth. The crown of the plant from where basal shoots grow should be just below the surface. If there is a soil mark on the plant, it should be kept about half an inch below the surface. A trowel or a spade is ideal for making holes in the ground.

If there is any foliage on thc plant it is to be kept just above the surface. Now, after putting the plant in the hole, spread its roots properly and then press the soil around the root very firmly so that no air pockets are left. Fill the hole with soil, keeping the plant straight. After planting, the plant needs proper watering.

Perennials should be spaced about 6 to 8 inches apart if they are edging plants, 12 to 18 inches space is ideal for plants for mid-borders and 1 ½ to 3 feet for the back of the borders.

Propagation of Perennials

Propagation of perennials can be done by division of roots or by cuttings. Most of them can be raised from seeds also.

Propagation through division of roots is quite simple. Original roots are divided but each division should have one shoot and some roots. If the original roots become a big hard clump, it is better to retain the other roots which are younger and, therefore, more vigorous and free from disease. Daisies and heleniums can be propagated by division of roots.

Fig. 10. Preparing a shoot cutting from a lupin plant.

Propagation of herbaceous plants can be easily done by cuttings also. Delphiniums, lupins and phloxes are increased by stem cuttings. About 4 inches long shoots are severed from the plant and then cut out cleanly just below the joints. These cuttings are then inserted in about 1 ½ to 2-inch deep holes made in sandy soil. Then the whole bed is soaked with water. These cuttings are transplanted only when they give out sufficient roots.

Plants with comparatively thin roots like phloxes, anchusas, hollyhocks, etc., can be successfully propagated by root cuttings. Root cuttings are taken by lifting the plant during September-October and cutting the roots into 2-inch long pieces. These cuttings with thick roots are then inserted in the sandy soil, right way up and fully covered with soil. At the time of cutting roots, the top end should be marked.

Thin root cuttings are laid horizontally on a sandy bed and covered with a thin layer of soil. Bed should be watered moderately till the shoots are grown, and then transplanted in a nursery bed.

Herbaceous perennials can be propagated by yet another method, that is from seeds. This is a relatively cheap but slow method. Usually plants raised from seeds differ widely from their parent plants but are vigorous and healthy. Perennials with a relatively short life like hollyhocks, lupins, etc., can be raised successfully from seeds. Usually, perennials raised from seeds bloom in their second year.

Perennials increased by divisions, bloom in their first year. But cuttings take a longer time and bloom in their second year.

Stem or root cuttings are vigorous plants and carry over less disease from parent plant. Cuttings taken even from infected plants produce healthy stock.

For selected varieties, perennials should be propagated by cuttings or divisions only as all the characteristics of parent plants are preserved.

After-care

After-care of herbaceous perennials does not take much time as they suffer from very few pests and diseases. Soot can be spread around the plants as a deterrent.

Faded flowers should be removed and, excepting evergreen plants, all the rest should be cut off upto an inch above ground level in autumn. This treatment will keep the bed clean and clear for hoeing.

A herbaceous border does not need any attention during its first year. Regular hoeing with a trowel is necessary to keep out the weeds and to loosen the soil.

Regular feeding with fully rotted animal manure or garden peat is desirable.

Top dressing with a fertilizer also helps the plants to grow well. About 100 grams of bone-meal per each square yard should be given as an additional manure.

After the first flowering season, plants should be provided with mulch, which is wet leaves and straw, in autumn, and then dug into the roots in spring.

Usually perennials need not be thinned or divided for the first 4 years or so but some free-growing plants like daisies or delphiniums need drastic thinning during the second year after planting.

If plants grow too vigorously and form clumps of ever-increasing size, replant them by retaining only the younger, outside portions of the clumps.

While replanting, herbaceous borders can be rearranged, lending a new look to the garden.

Plants with too many shoots overcrowd the bed, so only five or six shoots on each plant should be left. The rest should be severed to provide growing space. Finer flowers are produced on fewer shoots.

Staking of perennials is important but supports should be kept as inconspicuous as possible. They may be painted moss-green in colour and the plants should be tied gently with green string. Plants of medium height manage well with bushy branches or natural twigs, which are later hidden from view with plant foliage. Tall plants like delphiniums and double daisies need about 4 stakes each to prevent the plants from bunching tightly, which happens if only one stake is used for each plant.

Cannas are hardy perennials and make a good display in a large garden as they require plenty of room. In a small garden, grouping of a few plants is quite effective.

Cannas are mostly propagated by division of roots and are planted in July. They require a rich soil, so a trench is dug a spade deep and stable manure is mixed in the trench soil. Rhizomes of cannas are planted about 2 feet apart and 6 inches deep. Cannas planted in July bloom from October to December. Between April and June is their next blooming season. All dead flower-heads should be severed immediately and regular hoeing should be done to extend the flowering period of cannas.

Cannas need an annual rest for better results. Plants are lifted out in June and their rhizomes are kept buried in sandy soil in an open shed. Beds are dug and fed-in the mean time during this annual rest of rhizomes for one month.

Cannas produce blooms in several colours including orange, yellow, white and pink.

Perennial Climbing Plants

Climbing plants are usually planted to stay, and so are the permanent features of a garden. A site should be selected carefully for them, and preparation ofthe soil must be thorough.

Whatever kind of climber is planted, it needs adequate root

room, so a bed is dug quite deep and then filled with fully decayed compost. A few climbers like ivies or *Clematis* need a sprinkling of lime as well. Drainage should be good so that too much of moisture does not kill the plant. After preparing the bed, it should be left for a fortnight to settle.

Climbing plants are supplied in pots by the nurseries. After knocking the plants out and removing the crocks, some of the roots should be disentangled by moistening them with water. At the time of planting, these roots should have enough room to spread according to their natural growth. Any soil mark on the plants is kept about 2 inches below the surface. Soil around the roots is pressed and then the hole is filled and trodden down firmly around the plants.

Staking and tying of climbers are very important. Instead of nailing them to walls, train them to climb on trellis. Some climbers have their own tendrils and suckers and so are self-climbing like ivies. Such climbers quickly cover a wall or a screen. For arches etc., raffia or green string is used to fasten the climbers.

Regular top dressing and annual mulching is required to keep the climbers in good shape.

Pruning of climbers is done immediately after flowering. Overcrowded plants do not produce good blooms. *Clematis* is pruned quite severely to keep it within bounds.

Some of the climbers bear scented flowers and some of them have several flushes in a year.

Clerodendrun splendens and *Jacquemontia pentantha* are ideal climbers for shady places.

Chenomorpha macrophylla, J. officinale and *Jasminum grandiflorum* are some of the scented flower-bearing climbers.

Bougainvillea, *Clitoria ternatea*, *Jasminum sambac* etc., have several flushes in a year.

Bougainvillea, *Begonia venustc, Clematis flammula, Aspanagus sprengeri*, and monstera etc., can be grown in pots as well as in small gardens.

Climbing roses are ideal for arches or pergolas and can quickly cover an unsightly wall.

Most of the climbers are propagated by cutting or layering.

Biennials

Biennials differ from annuals in that they take more than one year to complete their growth circle. Their seeds are sown one year, to flower the following year.

Biennials resemble annuals in getting raised from seeds and dying after flowering and producing seeds.

Usually perennials are treated like biennials. Wall flowers are the best example. If left, they keep alive and flower for many years. But gardeners sow their seeds one year, to get flowers the following year, and then they are destroyed. Sweet Williams, forget-me-nots, hollyhocks, double daisies and foxgloves are fine examples.

Biennials need beds reserved for them for raising them from seeds and then for transplanting. Biennials may remain in their reserve beds till the plants are quite big.

Seeds of biennials are sown during September-October in straight rows. This way the seedlings cannot be mistaken for weeds and pulled out.

Seedlings are transplanted into nursery beds which should be situated in a sheltered position and rich in soil. The transplantation of seedlings is done when there are at least three pairs of true leaves. The distance between them should be about 9 inches to 1 foot so that the plants get plenty of space to develop. Hoeing is done regularly to keep the weeds away. Regular watering is also required.

Final planting of biennials is done in February-March.

Wall-flowers are very pretty biennials. They are raised from seeds sown at the end of February. Seedlings are transplanted during rainy season because this plant requires a lot of water. At the time of plucking out seedlings, as much of the original soil should be retained around the roots as possible. Soil should be firmly pressed around the roots at the time of planting.

A wall-flower is a bushy plant with a lot of foliage and a shallow rooting system. It has various colours. This plant requires soil with a little garden lime mixed in it.

Sweet Williams require a little lime in the soil. They are raised from the seeds sown in September-October and have flowers in various colours. They last longer as cut-flowers.

Forget-me-not (*Myosotis*) is planted in mass, to make a pretty display.

Foxgloves, polyanthuses, hollyhocks and double daisies are some other biennials. Pansies make a nice display, if grown as biennials in a rich soil. An open position or even a partially shaded place suits pansies. Violas also grow well in similar treatment.

CHAPTER 6

Annuals

Annuals are strictly for adding beauty to a garden and can be germinated from seeds. They flower, produce seeds and die, all within a few months and can be reproduced the following year with their own seeds. Seed sowing time for most of the annuals is the beginning of spring.

Seasonal display of annuals add beauty and colour to any garden. There are certain annuals grown for foliage only, which are usually raised during the summer and rainy season.

Soil for annuals should be well drained and well manured. Heavy soil becomes too wet when watered, so it is not suitable for annuals. Addition of sand and leaf-mould improves the soil.

Soil made too rich with quick acting fertilizers is not suitable for annuals as leaves of such plants become healthier than the flowers.

Flower-beds for annuals should be dug a week in advance, so that the soil soaks in sunlight and air. The surface of a seed bed should be firm and dry so that it does not sink at certain spots after sowing the seeds or seedlings.

Seeds for annuals can be sown in beds or in pots first. In beds they are sown either in shallow drills or broadcast.

Seeds sown in drills are a better method for borders. Broadcast method is good for irregular groups and patches. This method is more effective with such plants which cannot be successfully transplanted. Poppies and godetias are a fine example. Seedlings of such plants are thinned out as overcrowding makes the plants weak.

Different methods of seed sowing are given in detail in the chapter "Propagation of Plants."

Seeds for annuals should be bought from reliable firms. If seeds are collected from the previous year's annuals, they should be stored in a dry place. A single variety may have many colours, so all seeds should be stored separately and systematically.

Annuals should be arranged in beds according to their height and colour. Flowering period of annuals can be prolonged if all the dead flowers and seed heads are removed. Taller varieties of annuals need supporting with bamboo sticks.

Flowering Annuals for Winter

Annuals sown in September-October on the plains bloom in winter. Some annuals are sown in March-April on hill stations. They bloom in summer there.

Acroclinium *(Helipterum roseum)*

Flowers of this plant last for a long time and can be dried successfully for dry flower arrangements. This plant grows upto one foot and bears pink, cream and white flowers. Plants should be planted 6 inches apart.

For drying, flowers should be cut before they are fully developed and hung upside down. They need stem-wiring.

Ageratum

Ageratum is suitable for edging if the dwarf variety is sown, which grows, upto 6 inches only. It bears bluish flowers. Seedlings are sown 6 inches apart. Varieties upto 18 inches high are also available.

Alyssum (Alyssum marifimum)

Alyssum is a low plant, growing upto 4 inches only. Because of its height, it is a favourite edging plant, bearing yellow, pink, and white flowers. It is sown in December-January and blooms in March-April. Seedlings are transplanted 2 inches apart into shallow boxes and then finally in beds, 6 inches apart. Alyssum can be grown in the shade as well as in sunny places.

Anchusa (Alkanet)

Anchusa grows upto 18 inches in height and bears blue coloured flowers. Its seedlings are not transplanted and so should be sown where they have to grow. Anchusa seeds are sown in September-October about 8 inches apart. A sunny position is more suitable for anchusa plants.

Antirrhinums (Snapdragon)

Antirrhinums are of three varieties – tall, medium and dwarf and grow 6 inches to 3 feet high. Seeds should be sown thinly in September-October and seedlings transplanted 8 inches to 1 foot apart, according to the variety.

Central spike should be pinched off when it stops flowering. This way, side spikes are encouraged to flower, thus extending the flowering time. The dwarf variety does not produce a central spike. It also has a double flower variety and bears pink, white or crimson flowers.

Antirrhinum is often attacked by a disease called rust. Undersides of leaves get spotted and gradually wither. In such cases the plant needs spraying with fungicide.

Arctotis

Arctotis are also called 'African daisies'. They produce silvery-white flowers, with long stems. Seedlings are sown 2 inches apart in shallow boxes and transplanted in beds 1 foot apart. Arctotis need a sunny position and grow upto 2 feet.

Aster (Callistephims hortensis)

Aster has a double as well as a single variety. The aster is grown in open sunny positions and is excellent as a cut flower. Dampness does not suit seedlings so they should be transplanted soon. It is sown in September-October and keeps flowering till March. Seedlings should be sown 2 inches apart first and then finally 10 to 12 inches apart. Dead flowers should be removed. Sandy soil is suitable for growing asters.

Browallia

Browallia is raised from seeds sown in shallow boxes and then seedlings can be potted or sown in beds.

Browallis elata has smaller flowers which are excellent as cut flowers.

Calendula

This is one of the hardiest annuals and often reproduces itself from self-sown seeds. But these self-sown seedlings deteriorate in quality, so fresh seeds should be sown for either monsoon blooming in April-May or for winter blooming in October-November. Seeds can be sown outdoors and covered with ½ an inch of soil.

Seedlings are sown 9 inches apart. Plants grow upto 2 feet high and its flowers are yellow or orange in colour.

The winter flowering variety grows upto 8 inches to one foot. All dead blooms should be removed to lengthen the flowering period.

Californian Poppy (Eschscholzia)

Californian poppy is sown where it is to bloom as transplantation hurts its roots. It has poppy-like flowers in vivid yellow or red colour. It grows 9 inches to one foot tall and so seedlings should be thinned out to 8 or 9 inches apart.

Californian poppy blooms in poor soil as then foliage growth is less. Its seeds are sown in September-October and it blooms in December-January.

Candy Tuft (Iberis)

Candy tuft is sown for edging of flower beds and its flowers are white. Candy tuft can be sown in rock-gardens as well.

It grows in any kind of soil and is not transplanted but sown where it is to bloom. Its plants are about 6 inches to 9 inches high.

Carnations

Carnations are propagated by seeds sown in shallow boxes. They are finally transplanted outdoors. Carnation seeds are sown in September -October and they bloom in January-February. Carnations grow in pots also, and have the single flower as well as double flower varieties.

Chrysanthemum

Chrysanthemums can be grown as annuals from seeds. They

can be sown in light soil with very good drainage. Seeds are sown in drills about one foot apart and in beds where they are to bloom. Chrysanthemum has several varieties with single and double flowers.

Clarkia *(Clarkia elegans)*

Seeds of clarkia are sown where they are to bloom as its plants do not transplant well. They grow in nearly any soil in sunny as well as in partially shaded position.

Clarkia has double flowers of pink or red colour and plants are about 18 inches to 3 feet tall.

Cornflower *(Centaurea cyanus)*

Seeds of cornflower are sown in September-October in the beds where they are to bloom. Its seeds are sown thinly in drills about 9 inches apart for the small variety and 18 inches for the tall one. Tall variety needs some support. Dead flower heads should be removed to lengthen flowering time.

Cornflowers are excellent as cut-flowers.

Dahlia

Dahlia can be propagated by seeds as well as by root division and by cuttings.

There are many varieties available in dahlia, differing in height as well as in shape and colour of the flower. The tall variety grows upto 3 to 5 feet; the dwarf one usually only 18 inches to 2 feet.

Dahlia requires fairly rich soil to grow. Seeds are sown indoors in shallow pots and then seedlings are transplanted about 3 inches apart and then finally about one foot apart. Dahlia is potted singly.

Over-rich soil for dahlia encourages too luxuriant foliage growth, affecting the flower growth.

Tubers are stored in a dry place. The foliage is cut off and about 4 inches of the main stem is left with the tuber. Tubers should be sprinkled with flowers of sulphur and stored. Then they are planted in beds in August-September and a number of shoots will appear at the stem-base. These shoots should be detached with a portion of tuber and planted separately. If quite a lot of plants are required, then cuttings of only 2 inches of shoots are taken, leaving behind at least a couple of buds, which in turn give out more shoots for cuttings.

Propagating dahlias by cuttings is quite easy. Cuttings are taken as for soft-wood cuttings and planted. Cuttings should be at least 3 inches long.

For large flowers only one bud on each stem is retained. Dead flower-heads are also immediately removed.

Daisy *(Bellis perennis)*

Daisy can be propagated by division as well as by seeds. The common garden variety is used as an edging to flower beds. It is sown outdoors in nursery beds. The giant variety is finally sown 9 inches apart and the dwarf variety 6 inches apart. Seeds of daisy are sown in September-October.

Swan River Daisy *(Brahycome iberidfolia)*

This is an African variety of the daisy and it has white, pink or blue flowers. Seeds can be sown outdoors and seedlings are planted 6 inches apart. This is usually 6 to 9 inches high.

Dianthus

Dianthus plants are also called Fairyqueen and are about 9 inches high. The flowers come in mixed colours. Seeds are sown in August-September and seedlings are transplanted about 9 inches apart. Dianthus makes a good border plant.

Felicia

Felicia plant has daisy-like flowers. Seeds are sown in September October and plants start flowering by December-January.

Felicia has several species and it flowers in abundance. Seedlings are transplanted 9 inches to one foot apart and the height of the plant is usually one foot only.

Flax *(Linum)*

The annual variety of flax is about one foot high and is propagated by seeds. Flax seeds are sown where the plants are to flower and then seedlings are thinned to 6 inches apart. Flax grows in ordinary soil in a sunny position. It has sprays of scarlet flowers which do not last long. But this plant keeps on flowering for a long period, if dead flowers are removed.

Foxglove *(Digitalis purpurea)*

Foxglove needs a sunny or semi-shade place for good growth. Its plants are about 4 feet high and need staking.

Seeds are sown in August-September and seedlings transplanted about 6 inches apart and then finally 15 inches apart by December and they start flowering in July-August. Foxglove has white and purple flowers.

Godetia

Godetia is a very hardy annual as it can survive in any kind of soil and flourishes in either sunny or shady position. Godetia has tall, medium or dwarf varieties. Flowers are usually pink or magenta in colour.

The tall variety of godetia is about 2 to 3 feet high with spikes of flowers. The medium and dwarf varieties have bushy plants with flowers in clusters. Dwarf type is only about 6 to 8 inches in height and medium type plant is usually 15 inches high.

Seedlings of godetia cannot be transplanted because they have tap roots. Seeds are sown broadcast where the plants are to flower and then seedlings are thinned to 6 inches apart. Sowing time is September-October and flowering time is December-January.

Helichrysum *(Strawflower)*

Helichrysum is a hardy annual which is about 2 to 3 feet high. Its seeds are sown in September-October and seedlings are planted about 9 inches apart in an open, sunny position. Helichrysum flourishes in well drained soil and its seeds may be sown broadcast also and then seedlings are thinned to 9 inches apart.

It bears flowers with straw-like petals which can be dried and used for dry-flower decoration. For this purpose, flowers are plucked just before they are fully developed and hung head downwards in an airy place. Helichrysum flowers resemble double daisy flowers and are of bright yellow, pink or scarlet colour.

Hollyhock *(Althaea)*

Hollyhock plants can be raised from seeds as well as from root cuttings. Seeds are sown in drills $^1/_2$ inch deep and 6 inches apart in nursery beds and seedlings are firstly planted one foot apart and then finally transplanted 2 feet apart in flower beds.

Hollyhock is treated as a perennial as well as biennial plant. It flourishes in not too rich soil, in a sunny position and keeps flowering for many months, if dead flowers are removed immediately. When a hollyhock plant stops flowering, its main stem should be cut off by 6 inches. New shoots will appear soon and the plant will flower again.

Hollyhock is a tall plant and it grows upto 6 feet. It has long spikes of either single or double flowers in pink, white or maroon shades.

Larkspur *(Delphinium ajacis)*

Larkspur has large flower spikes in white, pink or blue colours. Its plants are about 2 to 3 feet tall and require well-drained soil. Seeds of larkspur are sown in nursery beds in August-September and seedlings are transplanted about one foot apart.

Larkspur starts flowering in November-December and makes a good cut-flower.

Leptosyne

Leptosyne is about an 18-inch - tall plant with yellow daisy-like flowers. It grows well in a sunny position in airy, ordinary soil.

There is a tall variety which has yellow dahlia-like flowers. Leptosynes are excellent as cut-flowers.

Lobelia *(Lobelia erinus)*

Lobelia is popular as an edging plant for flower beds. It grows in sunny as well as in semi-shaded position and can be grown from seeds sown in nursery beds or boxes. Seedlings are then planted about 2 inches apart and finally outdoors about 6 inches apart. Its flowers are mostly blue.

There is a trailing type lobelia available which is known as L-tenuior. This variety is ideal for hanging baskets or window boxes.

Love-in-a-mist *(Nigella damascena)*

Love-in-a-mist is another annual which grows on hills. It has a fern-like foliage and its flowers are of pink, white or blue. The plant is usually 18 inches high but its dwarf variety is only 9 inches high. Seeds are sown in March in the flower beds where the plants are to grow and seedlings are thinned out to 9 inches apart.

Nasturtium *(Tropaecolum majus)*

Nasturtium can be grown very easily from seeds. They flourish more in poor soil but in a sunny position. Even a semi-shaded place suits them. Seeds can be sown singly in small pots or in shallow boxes 2 inches apart.

Nasturtiums have round leaves and mostly yellow or orange flowers. Tall, medium and dwarf varieties are available. Tall and medium varieties should be planted one foot apart and dwarf variety 6 inches apart. Nasturtium is an excellent bedding plant and some unusual shades like pink, orange-pink and cherry are also available in nasturtiums.

Nemesia *(Nemesia strumosa)*

Nemesia plants are about 6 to 12 inches high and are most suitable for pots. They can be grown from seeds sown in a shallow box. The seedlings are transplanted into shallow boxes 2 inches apart. Nemesia needs extra rich soil in seed boxes as well as in flower beds. Sunny or semi-shaded position suits them and they need plenty of water.

Nemesia flowers are trumpet-like and grow in clusters, and are available in various colours.

Pansy

The pansy is actually a perennial plant but it is usually treated as an annual. It is raised from seeds annually as well as by cuttings. Seeds are sown either in nursery beds or sown broadcast where the plants are to grow. Seedlings are finally planted or thinned out 6 inches apart.

Pansy plants are very much similar to violas. Pansy flowers are strongly marked with black on various shades including yellow, purple and white. It requires very rich soil and a sunny position and plenty of water in dry weather.

Petunia

Petunia is grown from seeds sown in shallow boxes and seedlings transplanted into flower beds 9 inches apart. Petunia plant is about 1 foot to 18 inches high with flowers in white, pink and purple colours. It flourishes in rich, well drained soil. A dwarf variety of petunia is also available which is only 9 inches high. Petunia is a good pot-plant.

Phlox (Phlox drummondii)

Phlox has various species including perennials and herbaceous, but here we will describe the annual phlox only. It is about 6 to 15 inches in height and produces flowers in various colours including white, pink, crimson, mauve, etc. Phlox flowers grow in clusters. Phlox is grown successfully from seeds sown in shallow boxes. Seedlings are planted again in boxes 2 inches apart and finally transplanted 9 inches apart in flower beds. Phlox grows well in pots also.

Indian Pink (Dianthus sinensis)

Annual pink flourishes in sunny, well-drained soil. It is grown from seeds sown in shallow boxes. Seedlings are transplanted into flower beds about 6 inches apart. Its flowers are either single or double and in various shades of crimson or maroon with white blotches. The number of shoots should be reduced if larger blooms are desired.

Poppy *(Papaver rhoeas)*

Annual poppy plants like sunny and well drained position. Its seeds are sown broadcast where they are to grow and later thinned out to 9 inches apart. The plant grows upto nearly 2 feet with delicate double or single flowers.

If the poppy flowers are gathered, stem ends should be charred immediately, otherwise flowers die very quickly. A drop of wax dropped in the centre of the flower keeps the petals together.

Scarlet Salvia *(Salvia splendens)*

Perennial salvia is propagated by cuttings but mostly it is treated as an annual plant which is grown from seeds sown in nursery boxes. Seedlings are potted singly in very small pots, later on they are transferred to 4 inch pots and finally to flower beds. A warm, sunny position and any ordinary soil suit salvia. Its plant is about 18 inches high and it produces flowers in long spikes of scarlet colour.

Statice *(Sea-lavender)*

Statice is available in both perennial and annual varieties. The annual statice is called *Limonium sinuatum*. Statice is grown from seeds, and seedlings are planted 9 inches apart. Its plant is 18 inches high and its flowers are in various colours including pink and yellow and have a papery texture.

Statice flowers can be dried by cutting them with long stems just before the flowers are fully open and hanging them, head downwards, in an airy, dry place. These flowers retain their colour even after drying.

Ten-Week-Stock *(Matthiola incana)*

The ten-week-stock is the most popular variety. It is raised from seeds and is an ideal plant for pots. The plant grows 1 foot to 2 feet high and bears flowers mainly in mauve, pink and purple colours.

Virginian Stock *(Malcomia maritima)*

Virginian stock is a very pretty annual which requires very little care. It can grow in any corner of the garden or between the paving stones, where no other plant can grow.

Virginian stock is only 6 inches high. It is grown from seeds which are scattered where the plants have to grow. Seeds are then covered with a thin layer of sifted soil.

Sweet-Pea *(Lathyrus odoratus)*

Sweet-peas are the most popular of all the annuals, both as cut-flowers, as well as for garden decoration.

Sweet-peas do not require special care or soil. They grow in any soil. But for exhibition purposes, sweet-peas need some extra care. The ground in which they are planted, is prepared thoroughly by digging deep and mixing in well rotted animal manure and wood-ashes. Sometimes a 1 foot wide bed is prepared for holding two rows of sweet-peas. But this narrow strip should not turn into a drainage trench for the surrounding ground, otherwise plants will perish with too much of water.

Sweet-peas are grown from seeds sown singly in drills about 6 to 9 inches apart with a distance of 1 foot between the rows. Another method is to sow the seeds in shallow boxes or pots and then transplant them outdoors in beds. Tips of seedlings are pinched when they are only a few inches high or have three pairs of leaves, to encourage the plant to produce side-shoots.

Staking of sweet-peas is essential at an early stage before the plants begin to bend and get weakened at vulnerable points. Each plant may be given an independent stake at least 6 feet high. Another method of staking is to put in strong stakes at each end of the rows and put a few lighter stakes in between. Now a thin wire or nylon string is stretched horizontally at 6 inch intervals between these stakes.

For exhibition purposes, sweet-peas need extra rich soil. After the seedlings are pinched, and when they are a few inches high, plants give out many shoots. Only the strongest is retained. All side growths including tendrils are pinched out. Even the buds are removed if they appear too early or if the plants are not yet 3 feet high. If the plants reach the top of the stakes, they are carefully untied, laid on the ground for a few feet and then tied to another stake further along the row.

Sweet-peas need liquid manure every week after they start flowering. Before this a top dressing of animal manure is required once every fortnight.

Dead flowers if removed immediately prolong the flowering period.

Many varieties of sweet-peas are available. in various colours including mauve, purple, pink and white.

Sweet Sultan *(Centaurea moschata)*

Sweet sultans are excellent as cut-flowers and for flower beds and borders.

Seeds are sown where the plants are to grow and seedlings are thinned out 9 inches apart. September-October is the time for seed sowing and December-January is the flowering time.

Sweet sultan requires a well-drained soil and sunny position. Its flowers resemble cornflowers in shape. Sweet sultan flowers are in yellow, mauve or purple colours. Its plants are usually 18 inches high.

Sweet Williams *(Dianthus barbatus)*

Sweet William belongs to the family of pinks and carnations. It is a perennial and is grown from seeds sown in drills outdoors. Sweet Williams flourish in any soil but preferably well-drained and in sunny position.

Sweet Williams are 9 inches to 2 feet high according to their variety and flowers are in pink or red colour. Sweet Williams are nice as cut-flowers.

Toadflax *(Linaria vulgaris)*

The annual variety of toadflax is about one foot tall and has snapdragon-like flowers on slender 12 inch long spikes.

Toadflax is grown from seeds sown broadcast in the flower beds where they are to flower. Seedlings are thinned to six inches apart. It flowers in very striking colours, including purple, red and bright pink. They make excellent cut-flowers.

Tobacco Plant *(Nicotiana affinis)*

The ornamental variety *Nicotiana affinis* for the gardens grows well in hill stations. Seeds are sown in March and seedlings are first planted in boxes, then 3 inches apart, and then transplanted in flower beds or potted singly in May. *Nicotiana* plant is 1 foot in height and accepts any ordinary soil and sunny or semi-shaded position. Its flowers are long, tubular with wide mouths.

Ursinia

Ursinia is a daisy-like flower. It is grown from seeds which are sown either in pots and boxes or directly in the flower beds where they are to grow. Seedlings should be planted 9 inches to

1 foot apart so that they make a better display.

Ursinia plants require a well drained soil and a sunny position and are 1-2 feet high.

Venidium

Venidium belongs to South African daisy family. This plant is 18 inches to 3 feet high and is grown from seeds sown in nursery beds or pots. Any kind of soil suits them.

Verbena

Verbena is a perennial plant and can be multiplied by cuttings. But usually verbena is treated as an annual and is raised from seeds every year.

Verbena requires same treatment as antirrhinums. Its plant is sown 9 inches apart. It completely covers the ground and makes an excellent display in pink, scarlet and white colours.

Summer and Monsoon Flowering Annuals (sown in April-May)

Amaranthus *(Amaranthus caudatus)*

Amaranthus is a bushy plant which flowers in summer and monsoon. Its height is 2 to 3 feet and it can be raised from seeds sown directly in flower beds and later thinned out to 9 to 12 inches apart.

Amaranthus requires a rich soil and sunny position.

Indian Balsam *(Impatiens glandulifera)*

Balsam flowers in summer as well as in monsoon. Seeds are sown in shallow boxes or nursery beds and seedlings are planted at a distance of about 9 inches. Its plants are 18 inches to 3 feet high and have flowers in various colours including pink, scarlet, white, mauve and purple. Balsam has single as well as double flower varieties.

Balsam is potted singly.

Begonia *(Begonia semperflorens)*

Begonia is a perennial plant but is always treated as an annual. It is raised from seeds and seedlings are planted 2 inches apart in deep boxes. Finally begonias are transplanted in flower beds 8 or 9 inches apart. They can be potted singly.

Begonias require open and sunny position and leaf manure. Begonia leaves are either in green or bronze colour and flowers are white or scarlet and grow in sprays. Its plants are usually 9 inches high.

Celosia

Celosia comes in two different kinds. One is *C.Plumosa* which has plume like small flowers with silken sheen. It can be potted singly.

The other variety in celosia is cockscomb *C. Argenta cristata*. It has brilliant velvety flowers which grow in clusters with wavy ridges and look like a fowl's comb. Cockscombs are usually crimson or golden in colour.

Both the varieties of celosia are raised from seeds and make excellent pot plants. They need a sunny and sheltered position and plenty of water.

Gaillardia

Gaillardias require ordinary soil and a sunny position. Seeds are sown in nursery beds and seedlings transplanted 1-foot apart. The gaillardia plant is about 18 inches high and produces daisy-like flowers in various colours including crimson and yellow.

Ornamental grasses

There is a great variety available in ornamental grasses. They are grown from seeds sown where the grasses are to grow and seedlings are thinned to 6 inches apart.

These grasses grow well both in summer and monsoon and are good for potting.

Portulaca

Portulaca can be propagated from seeds as well as by cuttings. Its seedlings are transplanted about 1 $^1/_2$ inches apart.

Portulaca plants are a little bushy and are only about 6 inches high. They require light soil and sunny position. Its flowers are of various colours including magenta, scarlet, orange, white, yellow and pink. They are both of single and double varieties.

Sunflower *(Helianthus annuus)*

The sunflower plant sometimes grows upto 10 feet in height and bears large yellow flowers which contain large quantities of seeds.

Sunflowers are raised from seeds which are sown where the plants are to grow. Seeds are sown about 2 feet apart in twos or threes and later on the strongest seedlings are retained from each group.

Various varieties of sunflower are available and they differ in height. Some have double flowers of gaint size and some varieties have single flowers. But all sunflowers are in various shades of yellow only.

Sunflowers flourish in rich soil and sunny position. Its seeds start ripening after the flowers fade and flower heads should be cut before the seeds start falling.

Tagetes *(French and African Marigolds)*

Marigolds have a long flowering season and lend colour to the garden, especially during summer. Its flowers are single or double in orange or yellow shades.

Marigolds are raised from boxes, and seedlings are transplanted 6 to 9 inches apart, depending upon the variety. Seeds can be sown directly in the flower beds, where the plants are to grow.

Marigolds flourish in light, well-drained and rich soil. Those required for exhibition are grown singly in pots and are judged on the basis of the regularity of markings on the blooms. So seeds should be obtained from the plants with perfectly marked blooms.

Zinnia *(Zinnia elegans)*

Zinnias are excellent cut-flowers and are in various colours. They are very decorative for borders also. Some varieties of zinnias are double and some are single. Some zinnias have chrysanthemum-like quilled petals.

Zinnias flourish in rich and porous soil and require plenty of water and sun.

By two sowings, zinnias can flower in summer as well as in monsoon.

CHAPTER 7

Roses

Roses are an almost essential addition to large gardens, or even patch gardens. They seem to lend a distinctive look to any garden.

Roses can be grown on any kind of soil provided it is in a reasonably good condition. They grow well in open, airy space with no shade. Roses are supposed to be hungry plants which flourish with generous and regular feeding and pruning.

The most common type of roses in India are Hybrid Teas which produce either a cluster of roses on each stem or a big, shapely, single rose on each stem. This variety is a cross between 'Hybrid Perpetuals' and 'Hybrid Tea Rose'. Hybrid Tea Roses flower for a long time if dead flowers are immediately removed. After removal of dead flowers, the stalk should also be cut down upto the last shoot bud.

Another common variety of roses in India is Polyantha. It is a dwarf rose-bush and flowers in clusters.

Floribunda roses are similar to Polyantha roses but have larger flowers. This variety is suitable for flower-beds, borders and low hedges.

Climbing type of roses are a variety of Hybrid Teas.

Preparing the Rose-Beds

Rose-beds should be dug deep a few weeks before roses are to be planted.

All the soil taken out of the beds should be left to soak in sunlight and air for a couple of days. Now the deeply dug rose-beds are filled with well rotted animal manure or decayed leaves at the bottom. Top soil in rose-beds should not contain any organic manure as it harms rose-roots. If the soil is sandy, clay should be added.

The place in your garden for roses should be open and, airy. Roses should remain permanently at one place.

Planting of Roses

When rose plants are bought from nurseries, they should be unwrapped carefully so that no roots or stems are harmed. Then plants should be submerged in water. If they are in a very dry condition, they should be kept soaked in water overnight. Roses imported from England usually arrive in a more shrivelled condition. All the dead roots and shoots are carefully removed and plants are put in position in beds with their roots comfortably spread out. Soil should be thoroughly packed under rose roots and made firm with hands. Roses should be planted at a distance of about 2 ½, feet from each other. Plants should be planted at the same depth as they were planted at the nursery. The soil mark is easily visible. Plants should be thoroughly watered after planting is completed.

Planting is done during August-September in the plains only if heavy rains or a hot spell do not follow the planting. Otherwise successful planting can be done from the middle of October upto the middle of December. Pruning can be done within 2 weeks of planting.

Watering and Manuring

Good drainage is necessary for rose-beds. Too much of watering damages rose plants. The soil is kept moist but not wet.

After pruning, the whole rose-bed is top-dressed with leaf-mould, animal manure or bone meal.

When the plants starts flowering, about 10 grams of sulphate of ammonia is fed to each plant. It is applied a little away from the main stem and then a thorough watering of the plant should be done. This treatment encourages better flower growth.

Pruning

Pruning of rose plants is done in October but may be done earlier, if flowers are required earlier.

At the time of planting, roses are pruned and stems are cut down to the length of 3 or 4 inches. A stem which has just flowered, should be cut off so that the young stems give out flowers.

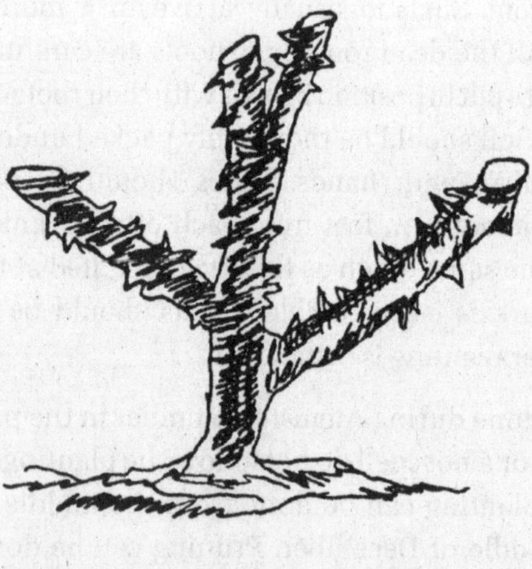

Fig. 11. Each strong growth is cut back to three dormant buds.

All dead and diseased branches are removed from the shrub roses at the time of pruning. Then strong branches are pruned.

There is a shoot bud pointing outwards away from the centre of the plant. This bud is usually third or fourth on the branch. A shoot is pruned just above this bud with a slanting cut.

Roughly, in all varieties of rose plants the strong shoots should be cut by half or two-thirds and thin shoots upto 3 or 4 inches.

Suckers

Often shoots grow from the base of the plant, which are called suckers. They have smaller and different leaves and if allowed to grow will give out wild roses. So suckers should be cut back to their base. These suckers arise from the main stem below the "budding point", where bud and stock are joined.

When cutting roses or removing dead flowers, stems of about 8 inches should be cut upto the last outwards pointing bud. This way more flowers are produced.

Roses need frequent weeding as weeds encourage diseases. There are various diseases which may attack rose plants.

Diseases

Red scale usually appear during August and September. All branches are covered with reddish brown insects. Rub the infected places with cotton soaked in methylated spirit. Spraying the infected plants with 0.1 per cent of parathion emulsion in April and October also helps to get rid of this disease.

Digger wasp gets into the plants from the pith of the newly pruned branches. These infected branches ultimately die. A mixture of equal parts of DDT and BHC applied to the pruned ends of branches prevents this disease.

White ants (termites) attack the plants from the roots, so soil in the pit should be treated with equal parts of BHC and DDT. One pit needs about 3 grams of the mixture. It can be applied as top dressing also.

Thrips are destroyed with phenyle and kerosene emulsion which is made by mixing 40 mls. of phenyle, 20 mls.of kerosene and $2^1/_2$ kgs. of soap suds.

Green fly can be destroyed with ordinary soap water or a small amount of tobacco leaves boiled in soapy water.

Caterpillars should be hand-picked. They are usually found under young leaves which get curled due to caterpillars.

Mildew is another fungus disease which attacks roses. It can be controlled by dusting with flowers of sulphur.

Black spot is the worst enemy of roses and attacks the leaves. Leaves start dropping, leaving the plant bare. All these fallen leaves should be burnt. Spraying with lime sulphur or fungicide controls the disease.

Fungicide can be prepared by mixing 2 parts of copper sulphate, 1 part of quick lime and 2 parts water. This solution should be kept in earthenware pots and should be stirred before use.

Canker disease which affects the twigs, ultimately kills the whole plant. Spraying with fungicide prevents it.

Pruned ends of roses should be covered with a mixture of equal parts of copper sulphate, red lead and linseed oil to get rid of **die-back disease** which starts with pruned ends. It turns the branches black and slowly kills the whole plant.

Propagation of Roses

Roses are propagated by budding and cuttings. Roses raised from seeds are rarely true to type as one plant in thousands comes out with sufficient merit.

Propagation by Cuttings

Roses are increased by cuttings taken in the month of October or in autumn. 9 to 12 inches long cuttings are taken from strong, young growths and are severed into the ground just below a joint. All the cuttings are inserted 4 inches into the ground, 9 to 12 inches apart in rows about 2 feet apart in a well drained bed.

Fig. 12. Disbudding a rose plant.

These cuttings do not require any further attention, except weeding.

Miniature roses are propagated by cuttings only. Budding cannot be done because of the thinness of their stems. Grafting is also done to increase them.

These cuttings can be used as stocks for budding.

Disbudding Roses grown for exhibition purposes require disbudding. This disbudding is done to Hybrid Tea varieties only and results in fewer flowers of a bigger size. All the buds, except the central one is rubbed out on each stem. (See Fig. 12).

Propagation by Budding

Buds are taken out of standard varieties of roses and even wild rose plants can be used as stock. A year-old-plant grown out of a cutting is used as stock.

Buds are 'growth buds' which are usually found in the angle made by the leaf stalk joining the stem.

Shoots bearing growth buds are severed from the plants. Then buds are cut from the shoots with a shield-like portion behind them. This process is described fully in the chapter 'Propagation of Plants' through a sketch.

The stock is prepared to receive the bud by making a T-shaped incision in the stem. Flaps of bark are lifted out with a sharp knife and the prepared bud is inserted in. Stock and bud are then firmly bound together with raffia. These buds root out and are severed to make separate plants. Upto 3 buds can be inserted on each stock. In case there is just one budding done on the main stem, the whole top growth is cut off so that the sap rising up is diverted towards the bud. This way a new rose plant is established more quickly.

CHAPTER 8

Layout of a Fruit Garden

Planning the layout of a small fruit garden is much more difficult than of a large plantation. Selection of various suitable varieties to ensure succession of fruits from a limited area, needs some careful planning.

Nearly all varieties of fruit trees thrive on well-drained loamy soil, but any soil, on which common vegetables like potatoes and tomatoes etc. can be produced, is capable of feeding fruit trees of nearly all kinds.

In small plots, trees can be planted without much planning except that same kind of trees should be close together. Underplanting of some vegetables can be done with success.

Bigger orchards need some symmetrical planning in planting fruit trees. Trees should be planted in straight lines with even spaces left in between.

A few specimens of each variety should be included in any orchard and planted close to each other. The main reason for this grouping is that most of the fruit trees are self-sterile, so they do not produce good crop or no crop at all, unless fertilised with pollen of another variety of the same type of fruit. Cherries, plums and to some extent apples and pears are self-sterile trees.

If there is a boundary wall, fruit trees can be planted along it, leaving at least 4 feet for the spreading of roots.

Planting

Soil preparation is very important before planting of fruit trees and should be done well in advance to allow the soil to settle down. Nearly all fruit trees need deep cultivation. Animal manure is well mixed in the soil and then coarse bone-meal and sulphate of potash are given as a top dressing. About 25 grams of sulphate of potash and 150 grams of bone-meal per square metre will be enough.

Soil should be crumbly and a little moist at the time of planting trees.

Holes for trees should not be so deep that roots get buried too deeply. There has to be enough room for the roots to spread out fully.

Stakes are driven in position, in the centre of the holes, before planting the trees, to avoid the risk of injuring the roots. The stakes should be long enough to support the trees during their first year.

Any damaged or decayed root is severed before planting.

Soil around the roots is made firm so that no air-pockets around the roots are left. To avoid injury to the bark, stems of the newly-planted trees are tied to the stakes with rubber covered strings.

Trees bought in their containers can be planted at any time of the year, provided the soil ball is kept intact and roots undisturbed.

Annual top dressing with well-rotted manure and 20 grams of potash per square metre is excellent for fruit trees.

Propagation

All fruit trees can be propagated by seeds, cuttings, grafting, and layering.

Plants raised from seeds are fit for serving as stocks upon which new or established varieties are grafted. Seedlings almost always differ from their parent plants and deteriorate in quality.

Plants raised from seeds take years to produce any fruit. So this method of propagation is not recommended for fruit trees.

Cuttings

Young growth, usually a year old, is taken for cuttings. These cuttings are either severed just below a joint or a side growth is pulled away from the main branch retaining a strip of the old bark. This "heel cutting" roots more easily. Cuttings should be about 12 inches long.

All these cuttings are inserted in well drained and well broken soil, about 12 inches apart. These cuttings take about one year to get well rooted and then they can be transplanted to their permanent place.

Grafting

Fruit trees are propagated by grafting. Scions for grafting are made from year-old growth and stocks are young, one-year-old fruit plants raised from seeds. A clean cut is made in the stock about 18 inches above soil level about one month before the grafting time.

Fruit trees need whip grafting which is fully explained in a separate chapter "Propagation of Plants".

Several scions can be made from a single branch, but tips of the branches used as scions should be discarded.

For converting older fruit trees to newer ones, rind grafting is done.

For rind grafting, scions are prepared as for "whip grafting" but stocks are prepared by cutting off main branches about 1 foot above the tree trunk, leaving behind thick stumps.

Then a vertical incision is made in the stock. The scion is prepared by making a sloping incision. Now bark from both sides of the incision, made in the stock, is raised with a sharp knife and the sloping side of the scion is inserted inside so that the cut surface lies against the stock. Two or three scions can be inserted in a stock if it is thick enough. Stock and scion are then bound together with a string and covered with polythene.

Budding

Propagation by budding is more suitable for stone fruits. Old trees cannot be revived by this method as only young shoots are suitable for budding.

Dormant growth buds are taken for budding. These are found in the angle where leaf stalk joins the stem. The lower portion of these buds is firm and hard. Leaves are removed from the selected shoots. "T" incision is made in the stem of a young tree about 18 inches above soil level. Flaps of bark from this "T" incision are lifted with a sharp knife and the bud is inserted inside. The bud is prepared off the tree with ½ inch of the bark retained at both ends of the bud. This shield-like portion is inserted inside the "T" cut in the stock and bound securely with raffia above and below the cut and covered with polythene.

After a few months the top growth of the stock is cut off just above the budding point. All side shoots on the stock below the budding point should be removed.

Layering

Layering is seldom used for propagating fruit trees. Stocks are raised from seeds. When seedlings are about a year old, they are cut back to a few inches. In the following spring, many side shoots will appear. Healthy shoots out of these are pegged down in the ground and properly covered with soil. These shoots throw out roots in the soil and can be separated from the parent plant.

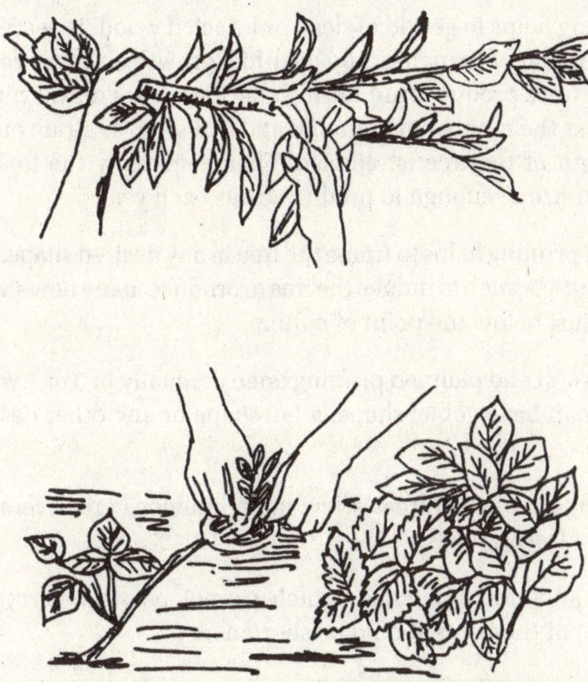

Fig. 13. Pruning of an apple tree is done by cutting soft ends of side shoots.

Pruning of Fruit Trees

The fruitfulness of a tree depends on correct pruning, so it should not be done haphazardly.

Fruit trees should be pruned immediately after planting. If two branches are growing out of the same point, the weaker one should be severed.

Pruning is done to allow fruits and leaves to get plenty of light and air. But during the first 3 or 4 years, pruning is done to form the frame of the tree according to the space available.

Pruning helps to get rid of dead or infected wood. It decreases the number of branches, and healthier growth and crop result. Some trees produce fruit during alternate years only. Pruning reduces the number of branches and fruits and so strain on the strength of the tree is reduced. Then eventually the tree becomes strong enough to produce fruits each year.

Initial pruning helps to frame the tree in any desired shape. You may cut a branch to induce the tree to produce many new shoots from just below the point of cutting.

By careful and planned pruning done gradually in 3 or 4 years, trees can have goblet-shape, a fan-shape or any other desired shape.

In well established trees a few main branches are severed to induce fresh growth.

Long and thin branches, which cannot possibly carry the weight of the fruits should be shortened.

Too many fruit buds put a strain on the tree and result in a weak crop, so the number of fruit buds should be reduced.

Sometimes pruning is done to encourage the formation of several fruit buds on one young shoot. Two shoots out of every six shoots are cut back to the length of an inch. The uncut branches form fruit buds more freely for nearly two years after which they are severed from the tree. Meanwhile the pruned shoots will develop stronger fruit buds.

Ringing

The bark of a tree is removed in a ring shape. This method forces the tree to be less vigorous and so produce more fruits. The flow of sap from the leaves to the roots is checked for a short time by this method. So root growth is checked and there is no need for root pruning. This method is not effective with stone fruit trees.

Ringing is done on individual branches also, to encourage growth of fruit buds, where previously they have not been formed. Pruning is never done during winter.

Root Pruning

Sometimes very vigorous growth of roots is checked by pruning, otherwise such trees have too much of growth at the expense of fruit.

Some of the roots are cut back by digging a trench around the tree a few feet away from the stems. Then roots are uncovered and thick ones are cut.

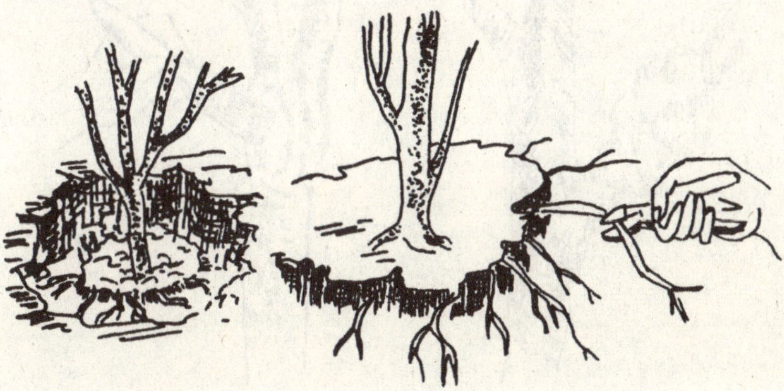

Fig. 14. Young trees are sometimes lifted out and roots pruned.

Spraying of Fruit Trees

Most of the spraying and dusting of the fruit trees is done as a preventive rather than as a curative measure.

Lime sulphur, tar-oil and derris powder are the least poisonous.

Tar-oil application on trees is done every second or third year only to rid the bark of moss, lichen and green scum.

Spraying with tar-oil should be done during the dormant period or till just before the buds begin to grow. It kills eggs of aphids, greenflies and scale insects. Vegetables and other plants growing under the fruit trees should be covered at the time of spraying. Rub your hands and face with lanolin before spraying.

Lime sulphur controls apple scab and red spider but it harms apple trees if sprayed after blossoms have formed.

Apples are often attacked by sawflies or codlin moths. Sawflies

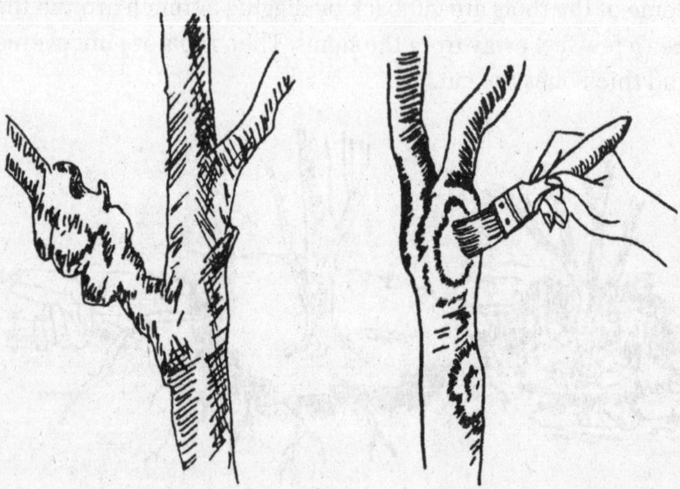

Fig. 15. Cut away the branches affected by canker and paint the wounds.

are destroyed with lime sulphur mixed with lindane. Codlin moth is controlled with derris of malthion sprays.

Raspberries are attacked by raspberry beetle and its flowers should be dusted with derris. When fruits are formed, they should again be dusted with derris.

To prevent greenflies and blackflies from infecting shoots and leaves, trees should be sprayed with malthion or derris. Canker often attacks apple trees and because of this disease, either the bark of the tree strips away or the wood starts decaying. The best preventive measure is to cut away the affected branches and paint the wounds.

Blossom wilt disease makes the blossoms wilt suddenly. All wilted portiors and branches should be removed.

Brown rot is also cured with surgery. It attacks trees during the blossoming period and fruit becomes brown and rotted. All infected spur or bark should be removed and burnt.

Caterpillars are small and are green or brown in colour. They attack newly-opened blossom buds and should be destroyed promptly by spraying with derris.

Cultivation of Fruit Trees

Apples

Apples are grown on hills. They require a well drained loamy soil. Heavy soil causes canker disease.

Nitrogen is an essential food for apple tree for its growth and potash is essential for fruitfulness. Well-rotten cowdung mixed with a little woodash is ideal planting soil for apple trees.

Most of the apple trees produce a much better crop when they get pollen from another variety of apple tree, so apple trees of different varieties should be planted close to each other. Effective pollination period of any one tree is 5 or 6 days.

Planting of apple trees is done when its leaves begin to fall off. Trees grown in containers can be planted at any time of the year.

Apple trees should not be allowed to bear fruits during their first year. Its blossoms should be removed.

Pruning of apple trees is done after planting. They need heavy pruning during their first year to encourage healthy growth of the tree.

Sometimes trees are over-laden with fruit. A little thinning should be done by removing the centre fruit on each cluster.

Apples are ready to be picked when they come off the stalks easily without tearing or twisting. All the fruits on a tree are not ready to be picked at the same time.

Banana

Banana trees are propagated by suckers growing out of underground stem.

Well-dug ground, manured with ammonium sulphate or calcium superphosphate is ideal for planting of banana trees.

Annual green manuring is required for good crop of bananas.

Ber

Ber tree grows even on dry lands and alkaline soil. It requires regular pruning and irrigation for better crop.

Ber ripens in January-February and is propagated by seeds or budding.

Guava

Guava requires a dry hot climate and is planted in sandy loam.

Guava is propagated by seeds, layering and suckers. Its trees are planted in July-August and do not need extra care.

Annual manuring is required and rotted animal manure is dug in around the tree.

Guava trees are available in different varieties and need light pruning.

Nimbu

Nimbu is propagated by seeds sown about 2 to 3 inches apart in summer. Seedlings are transplanted 6 to 8 inches apart. Finally, young trees are planted in one metre square holes filled with well-rotted manure.

Nimbu tree needs nourishment before flowering in the form of woodash, bonemeal, animal manure and a sprinkling of superphosphate.

Lime

Lime trees are propagated by seeds, layering and budding. It bears white flowers in clusters. Its fruits have a thin skin.

Lime does not grow well in high humidity.

Pomegranate

Pomegranate is small shrub-like tree which is propagated by cuttings. Pomegranate should be planted in a hole filled with well-rotted animal manure mixed with soil. Light pruning is required. 'Kandhari' is the best variety of this fruit and is often attacked by pomegranate butterfly. Fruits should be bagged individually.

Strawberry

Strawberry grows well in hilly areas but can be successfully grown in the plains also.

Well-drained sandy loam is ideal for growing this fruit.

Strawberries are propagated by seeds or runners. Each runner has many plantlets but only one nearest to the parent plant should be retained. Rest of the runners should be pinched off. Plantlets should be pegged down to the soil with a wire and after a few weeks, it will develop many roots. Then it can be severed from the parent plant and transplanted.

Plants should be planted in September about 15 inches apart. The uppermost roots should be just covered with soil. Distance between the rows should be about 2 $^1/_2$ feet.

Just before the plant flowers, straw should be spread under the plants so that later on the berries can rest on it.

Plants should be protected from birds and the fruit should be picked daily in the morning.

An annual mulching of cow-dung is required. Superphosphate of lime and sulphate of potash are also given to each plant annually in small quantities. 50 to 60 grams of each will be sufficient for one square metre.

Grapes

Grapes can be grown successfully even in a small garden. Its vines are trained into the walls and fences or onto pergolas.

Planting and Propagation Grapes need sandy loamy soil and good drainage. They are propagated by cutting and grafting.

Cuttings should be about 12 inches long and prepared from a year-old-growth which has just finished producing fruits.

These cuttings are severed just below a joint and potted singly in sandy soil in 3-inch pots, and after they develop enough roots, these cuttings are transferred to the place where they are to grow.

Grapes are propagated by layering also. Young stems are ideal for layering.

Potted vines are easier to transfer to soil without root distur bance, so if purchased from nurseries, they should be in pots.

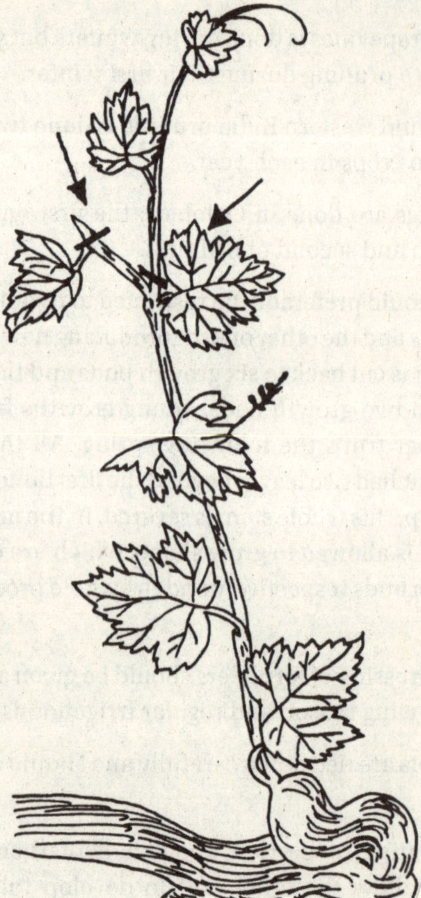

Fig. 16. Side growths are pinched two leaves bey flower bunch.

Roots should be disentangled with a sharp stick from the tight ball and spread carefully in a hole deep enough to cover the upper-most roots.

Grapevines are self-fertile and do not need various varieties for pollination.

Pruning of grapevines is done during winters but young plants do not require pruning during their first winter.

In southern and western India pruning is done twice a year as there are two crops in each year.

Both prunings are done in October : the first one before the October crop and second one after it.

Each vine should preferably be restricted to two stems, one for bearing fruits and the other one for producing new growth. The fruiting stem is cut back to six growth buds and the other stem is reduced to two growth buds. Young growths from the first stem will bear fruits the following spring. All these growths should be pinched two leaves beyond the first bunch of flowers. After the crop, this whole stem is severed. In the meantime, the second stem is allowed to grow shoots which are cut back to 6 and 2 growth buds respectively and the whole process starts all over again.

A good top-dressing of fertilizers should be given after pruning or in the growing season and regular irrigation is required.

All side shoots are tied down carefully and should not be pulled arshly.

fter the setting of berries, about half of them should be moved to allow the other half to develop fully. Thinning ould be confined to the interior of the bunch. If at all the rries on a bunch are allowed to grow, the size of fruits will not good.

If at the time of pruning, a cut surface starts bleeding – that is–starts throwing out sap, it can be stopped by charging the bleeding ends with a very hot iron.

Best varieties in grapevines are *Pusa Seedless, Kandhari* and *Anab-e-Shahi* etc., in Northern India. *Bangalore Purple, Thomson Seedless and Pachdarkshahi* in Southern India and *Anab-e-Shahi, Pandhari Sahetri, Bokhari, Thomson Seedless* and *Bangalore Purple* etc., in Western India.

CHAPTER 9

Layout of a Small Vegetable Garden

Growing various vegetables in a small garden and getting a good crop needs a bit of planning, and a knowledge of each vegetable's soil requirement, sowing time and cultivation methods.

A vegetable garden should be an open position with equally divided rectangular plots connected with irrigation channels. Vegetables need plenty of direct sunlight so plots should not be close to trees.

Crop rotation is done to maintain the balance of soil fertility. It means that same types of vegetables should not be sown at the same spot every year. So different crops are grown in rotation. Pests and diseases are also discouraged by the crop-rotation method.

It will be a more practical idea to divide the plot roughly into 3 sections namely A, B and C. In the first year, section 'A' should be allotted to root crops, section 'B' to brassicas and section 'C' to beans, peas, tomatoes, Lady's fingers (*Bhindis*) etc. In the second year, vegetables grown on section A should be sown on section B; vegetables sown on section C should be sown on section A and so on.

Inter-cropping is another method of getting the maximum out of a small vegetable plot. Two or more varieties of vegetables are grown on the same plot. For inter-cropping, the ground should be in an excellent condition. Peas, tomatoes or lady's fingers may accommodate lettuce, spinach or radish between their rows.

Successional cropping helps to have continuous supply of any one variety of vegetable. Seeds of desired vegetables like cabbage, cauliflower and lettuce etc., are sown at an interval of a fortnight to lengthen the time of harvesting.

Cash cropping is another way of getting the maximum out of a vegetable garden. No part of garden is left idle for any time of the year. Some quick growing vegetables like lettuce or spinach are sown in the bed prepared for potatoes or some other slow growing vegetables.

For regular supply of vegetables from your own garden a great deal of planning is required.

For a better layout of your vegetable plot, space for all the essentials should be properly allotted.

Seeds should be bought from reliable nurseries and should not be stored for the following year. Only fresh seeds give a good yield.

A small area is required for seed beds. This space should be utilised after all the transplantation has been done. Some space should be allotted for storing manures.

Good garden hygiene should be observed for a good turnover of crops.

All garden refuse should be dumped at one place and disease infected refuse burnt.

Well-rotted dung and compost should be the main soil for all the vegetables. Chemical fertilizers also help the vegetables to grow better. Potash, nitrogen and phosphates in equal quantities make a well blended fertilizer.

Regular hoeing allows moisture and air to reach the roots and keeps the weeds away.

Digging up your vegetable plot once or twice a year helps to expose pests.

The nature and amount of crops produced depend on various factors like good hygiene, suitable weather, quality of seeds, fertility of the ground and control of pests and diseases.

Nursery beds should be slightly raised for better drainage. The soil for raising seeds is: 2 parts garden soil, 1 part sand and 1 part leaf mould. The same soil mixture is good for pots also.

Seeds can be sown broadcast for all the vegetables but seeds sown in a line give out better results. Weeding and hoeing is also easier in line sowing. Thin or small seeds may be mixed in sand and then sprinkled on the prepared soil.

Seed-beds need regular and gentle watering. During summer small seedlings need protection against sunlight, so they may be covered with leaves.

When plants develop four true leaves, they may be transplanted and watered immediately.

Given below are a few brief directions for the vegetables likely to be grown in a small vegetable garden.

Beans

All types of beans are self pollinating and rich in protein, carbohydrate, Vitamin A and minerals. Beans take up the nitrogen of the air and assimilate it, so the soil gets an extra supply of nitrogen by digging in the bean roots.

Except French beans, all the other varieties of beans are vines.

Broad beans are chiefly sown for their seeds which are cooked as a vegetable.

French beans are basically bush plants although climbing plants are also available.

French beans are sown from August to September or even in February and mature in a short time. They can be grown on all types of soil but sandy soil gives an early crop. Lime is necessary in acid soil. It increases the yield.

French beans are sown in drills 9 inches apart, the drills being about 2 feet apart. The climbing variety of French beans needs staking but the bush variety does not need any support. Beans do not need much attention during their growing period, except hand hoeing to keep out the weeds. Regular irrigation is required; at the time of pod development, mulching with grass peat and straw helps.

French beans should be allowed to grow fast and gathered when they are about 3 $^{1}/_{2}$ inches in length. Beans allowed to get coarse and mature on the plants check further production.

Successive planting of french beans is done for continuous harvesting.

Jampa, Kentucky wonder, Contender and *Pusa parbati* are some of the improved varieties.

Cluster beans are produced on a bushy type of plant. They are sown in February-March in northern plains and in December-January in the southern plains. Farmyard manure is mixed in the soil beds for growing cluster beans.

Vegetable cowpea and **broad beans** etc. are some of the varieties in beans.

All varieties of beans are usually attacked by bean weevils, bean aphids and pod-borers. Powdery mildew, anthracnose bean-rust and bean mosaic are some of the diseases most likely to attack beans.

All these pests and diseases are discussed in a separate chapter.

Beetroot

Beetroots contain proteins, calcium, phosphorus and carbohydrates and are mainly used for salads.

Richly manured soil causes forking of the roots so the best soil for beetroots is one which has been well manured for a previous crop.

Beetroots, like all other root crops are sown during winter on ridges. Seeds should be sown 4 inches apart. Beetroot seeds are like capsules containing several seeds, so if many seedlings appear, they should be thinned out to 8 inches. If smaller and very tender beets are required, seedlings should not be thinned.

Crimson globe and Detroit dark red are the improved varieties of beetroot.

Leaf miners, web worms, etc., are pests most likely to harm beetroots. Spraying with parathion and DDT helps.

Leaf spot may attack beetroots. Leaves become spotted and finally turn grey. Spraying with Bordeaux mixture and crop rotation helps.

Brinjal *(Aubergine or Egg plant)*

Many species are available in brinjal and are there the year round. Mainly it is a summer crop not requiring any particular type of soil.

In northern India, 2 crops are produced. The first crop is sown in February and the second in July. In south India three crops of brinjals are produced in December-January, in June-July and again in September-October.

In acidic soil, liming is necessary for a good yield of brinjals.

These round or sausage-shaped fruits are harvested before they have fully ripened. Their skin should not lose the gloss and smoothness.

Brinjals are usually attacked by damping off or blight or virus of leaves and various pests like stem-borers or shoot-borers.

Pusa anmol, Pusa purple long and *Pusa purple cluster* are some of the improved varieties.

Cabbage

Cabbage is a winter vegetable, rich in vitamin A and C. Liming of the soil is essential if it is acidic, otherwise cabbages can be grown on any type of soil. The plot allotted to them should be dug deep and richly manured with farmyard manure.

Seeds of cabbages are sown in August, September and October. For successional harvesting, seeds are sown 6 inches apart and half an inch deep. Seedlings are transplanted 18 inches apart in rows and 2 to 3 $^1/_2$ feet distance is kept between the rows.

The best site for cabbage is the one which has been manured for an early crop of potatoes. In such cases no further manure is needed except potash and phosphates as fertilizers.

Cabbage crop needs regular hoeing and weeding. At the time of harvesting cabbages, a cross-cut should be made on cabbage stumps. Some stumps produce some growths for cooking.

Three months after sowing cabbages a top dressing of nitrate of soda should be given, 20 gms. of it mixed in water is enough for a 6-foot long row.

When seedlings are just coming out of the soil, they should be dusted with derris powder to control flea beetle. This application should be repeated again after a week. Leaf spot often attacks cabbages which can be checked by dusting with flowers of sulphur.

Caterpillars should be hand-picked and their eggs destroyed. These eggs are on the undersides of the leaves. Pests like aphids, root fly and diseases like clubroot are likely to attack cabbage crop. Heavily infected plants should be burnt and others dusted with derris.

Carrots

Carrots are one of the winter vegetables sown between September and January. Light soil is more suitable for the carrot crop, heavy soil needs more manure to make it porous for quicker germination. This crop is a heavy feeder and so needs farmyard manure as well as fertilizers.

If long carrots are desired, the soil should be dug deep and broken evenly.

Carrots need regular hoeing for better development of roots and for keeping out the weeds. Seeds should be sown in drills not more than an inch deep. Regular irrigation is needed and a light watering should be done before pulling out the carrots.

Carrots should be sown in fresh plots each year to avoid carrot fly which is very harmful.

Carrot fly lays its eggs in the soil near the carrots. Larvae feed on the carrot and heavily damage the crop. Sand soaked in paraffin can be spread along the carrot rows at the sowing time to deter the carrot fly. Naphthalene balls are also scattered fortnightly. Dusting with derris powder helps.

Cauliflower

Soil requirements for cauliflowers are the same as for cabbages. They require an open and sunny position and early varieties require sandy loam. This crop matures in a shorter time, so a rich soil and regular watering help. Dusting with superphosphate of lime a week before planting time helps produce a better crop. Early varieties of cauliflower are sown in June. The next sowing is done in July-August and late variety sowing is done in September-October. It can be grown with cabbages and knol-khol.

When curds on cauliflower begin to form, they should be covered with some inner leaves to protect them against sunlight and frost. Cauliflowers are cut when curds are fully formed.

Pusa Katki is an ideal early variety maturing in 60 to 80 days. *Aghani, Snowball* and *Giant Snowball* are the varieties sown in July-August. Late variety is *Dania Kalimpong*.

Cucumber

Cucumber needs a short time to grow and does not require a warm climate as it thrives well in the rainy season. It requires a sandy loam soil with good drainage. Its seeds are sown in January to March and again in June/July for rainy season crop.

Regular hoeing and weeding help the fruits to grow large. They are harvested when about 15 to 35 centimetres long. Some of the improved varieties are *Gemini, Straight Eight* and *China* etc.

Cucumbers are planted on slightly raised beds with flat tops. Male flowers are not pinched for fertility of female flowers. Sometimes male flowers are picked and shaken over female flowers for pollination.

Cucumbers should be watered freely otherwise the fruits become bitter on dry soil.

Garlic

A dozen plants of garlic are sufficient for a small vegetable garden. Garlic is propagated by cloves. Mild climate and light soil make the plants flourish. Its roots do not go deep, so only light ploughing is needed.

Garlic is planted in November in plains and in August in Andhra Pradesh. Its cloves are planted 6 inches apart in 1-foot apart rows and are barely covered with soil.

When the foliage turns yellow, the whole plant is lifted out and hung in a cool airy place. Some of these should be stored in a frost-free place for replanting next year.

Gourds and Pumpkin

Gourds and pumpkin are grown all over India and are rich in Vitamin A and C, minerals and carbohydrates.

Gourds and pumpkin need a long growing season. Rainy season suits them best. Too much of light gives rise to male flowers. They are grown in summer also. January to March is the right time for a summer crop, June/July is the time for a rainy season crop. Bottle-gourd, bitter-gourd, sponge or ridge-gourd, ash-gourd, and snake-gourd are the various varieties in gourds. All these can get cross-pollinated, so different varieties of gourds should not be sown together.

Knol-Khol

Knol-khol is a winter vegetable tasting like turnip. It is rich in minerals and Vitamin A and C. It is a cross-pollinated crop and requires same soil treatment as for cabbages and cauliflowers. They are harvested when about 5 to 7 centimetres in diameter.

Knol-khol is propagated by seeds sown along the cabbages in flat beds in drills, 9 inches apart. Seeds are sown in nursery beds and then transplanted.

Improved varieties are *White Vienna, Purple Vienna* and *Kyote No. 3*.

Among the common pests and diseases attacking this crop is whip-tail which makes the growth deformed but liming of the soil helps. Damping off, black-rot, leaf-spot and club-root are other common diseases. Saw fly and butterfly are other enemies of cole crops (cauliflower, cabbage, knol-khol).

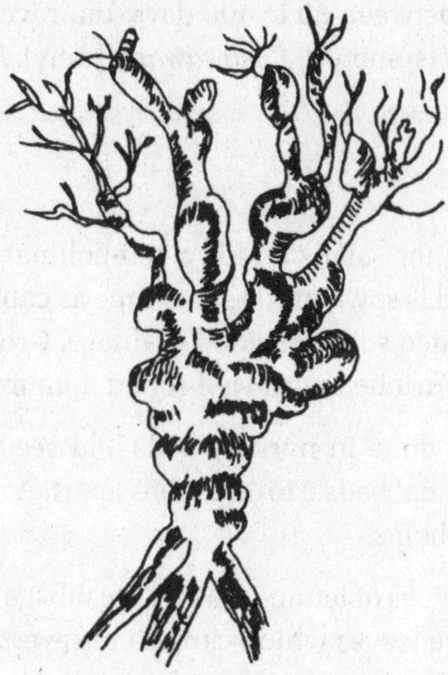

Fig. 17. Club-root disease.

Lady's Fingers *(Bhindi)*

Lady's finger is a warm season crop but can be grown throughout the year except during severe winters.

It can grow in any type of soil but gives better crop in light soil. Sandy loam is the ideal light soil for this crop.

The first sowing is done in January, second in June/July and third in September/October. In cold regions third sowing is not done.

Seeds are sown 6 inches apart and rows are kept 12 inches apart. For rainy season sowing, seeds are sown about 9 inches apart. Sowing is done in flat beds. It needs regular weeding and hoeing. Too much moisture harms the plants so bhindi should be irrigated every fourth day during summers and once a fortnight during winters.

Crop matures between 80 to 100 days. Improved varieties are *Pusa makhmali* (summer), *Pusa sawani* (rainy), *Red bhindi* and *IHR 20-31.*

Lettuce

Lettuce is used for salads and is a self-pollinated crop. It is a winter crop and is sown at the same time as cabbages. It needs rich, well irrigated soil with good drainage. Ground should be dug deep and enriched with well rotted manure.

Seed-sowing is done in nursery beds and seedlings are later transplanted in flat beds 8 to 12 inches apart. A light dusting of nitrate of soda helps.

There are two types of lettuce, one with cabbage like heads and other with loose leaves which can be cut several times.

Improved varieties are *Great lakes, Imperial 859, Slow bolt* and *Chinese yellow.* Downy mildew, mosaic and soft-rot are the diseases likely to damage lettuce crop. Aphids may also cause damage to this crop.

Mint

Mint requires an open, sunny position and reasonably rich soil. Root cuttings are inserted in beds in summer and regular hand hoeing is done to keep out the weeds. By the second year it has a dense growth from which shoots can be picked as required. Shoots are lifted in summers and replanted for fresh growth in manured ground.

Onions

Onions are propagated from bulbs or from seeds. Onions require mild climate and light soil, which can be either loamy or sandy. Shallow digging will be sufficient for onions.

October-November is the seed sowing time in northern plains in nursery plots and then transplanted 6 inches apart in rows 1-foot apart.

Bulbs are planted 6 inches to 1-foot apart. In southern India even three sowings of onions are done in June to October, October-January and then from January to June. Green onions are pulled out with hands when they are formed. Bulb crop takes about 3 to 5 months to mature and then most of its foliage gets yellow or dry. After a light watering the ready crops can be lifted out with khurpi or shovel and then tops are removed.

Early grane variety is suitable for green salad and matures in about 80 days.

Peas

Pea is a winter crop which is rich in proteins, carbohydrates and calcium etc. It is a self pollinated crop and can be grown on all types of soil but a light soil is ideal for an early crop.

The ground is dug deep and well rotted cowdung is mixed in the soil. Then before sowing the seeds, the bed surface is dusted with superphosphate of lime (about 60 gms. per sq. yd.) and sulphate of potash (about 30 gms. per sq. yd.).

Pea seeds can be sown either in flat beds 9 inches apart or in 2-inch deep and 9-inch wide trenches. Two lines of seeds are sown in each trench and seeds are covered with 1-inch of soil. This way a 1-inch depression will be left in the trenches for watering in dry weather. Seeds should be sown singly 2 inches apart.

Successional sowing is practised for continuous harvesting starting from October.

Peas crop requires moisture when pods are filling. 60 to 100 days are enough for the crop to mature and then pods are picked regularly to encourage further bearing.

Improved varieties are *Early badger, Bonneville* and *Sylvia* etc.

Varieties below the height of 2 feet need not be staked but others need some support which can be given with some branches staked in place when seedlings are only a few inches high.

Green Pepper and Chillies

Green peppers (Shimla mirch or capsicum) are grown in relatively mild climate whereas chillies are grown in the plains and are pungent. Green peppers are either mildly pungent or non-pungent.

Chillies are sown thrice in a year in plains and twice where severe winter occurs. These sowings are done between November and July. Seeds are sown in nursery beds and transplanted 12 to 24 inches apart.

Damping off and leaf curl virus are the diseases likely to harm the crop. Improved varieties are *California wonder, Polo wonder* and *N.P. 46-A*.

Potatoes

Potatoes are sown in September to November and are ready for harvesting by December or January. Potatoes need a loamy soil with well-rotted dung mixed in the soil. Before planting potato tubers, 80 gms. of fertilizer per sq. yd. should be dusted on the ground. This fertilizer should contain 5 parts of lime, 2 parts of sulphate of ammonia and 2 parts of sulphate of potash.

Potatoes are propagated by tubers known as seed potatoes, sown 12 to 15 inches apart in rows 3 feet apart and 3 inches deep. As soon as shoots appear, soil should be drawn over them. This process is repeated thrice at the interval of 15 days. Shoots should grow out of this.

At the time of harvesting, potatoes should be atleast as big as eggs. *Up-to date* and *Military special* are the suitable varieties.

Potato blight can be checked with the spraying of Bordeaux mixture.

Radish

Radishes are quick growing plants rich in vitamins A, B and C. They are excellent for inter-cropping and can be sown in between peas, cabbages or cauliflowers.

Radishes are either round or long, tap-rooted and are of winter season crop. Sandy-loam soil is best suited for radishes. They are sown in September to January. In southern India they can be sown in summers also.

Seeds are sown six inches apart in $^1/_2$-inch deep drills. Regular irrigation and weeding are required. Radishes are ready within 20 to 45 days.

Improved varieties are *Five-eight (desi), Japanese white, White icicle* and *Red white tipped.*

Aphids, saw fly, white rust and flea beetle are the common enemies of this crop.

Spinach

Spinach is a leafy crop which grows very quickly and is ideal for inter-cropping. Successional cropping can also be done.

It requires a deeply dug ground, thoroughly manured. Its plants need nitrate of soda at the rate of 40 gms. for a 20-foot row.

Spinach seeds are sown in one inch deep drill 4 inches apart. Outer leaves should be cut when required within four weeks of seed sowing.

Virginia savoy and *Early smooth* leaf are the improved varieties.

Spinach needs harvesting after every 15 days to avoid the formation of seeds.

Tomatoes

Tomatoes are sensitive to frost and grow well in warm season. They grow on all types of soil, and can give two to three crops a year, one in February and second in July in rains. In southern India tomatoes give out 3 crops in December, June and September respectively.

Excessive irrigation is harmful but soil should remain moist for tomatoes. Regular hoeing is essential. Staking of tomatoes is a must to avoid many diseases.

A top dressing of fertilizer containing sulphate of ammonia, superphosphate of lime and sulphate of potash and animal manure should be given when the fruit starts swelling.

Improved varieties are *Pusa ruby, Pusa early dwarf, Red and White tipped etc.*

Tomatoes may be attacked by damping off, early blight, fruit rot, powdery mildew, leaf spot or sun injury disease.

Turnips

Turnips are quick growing plants and, if not checked, will produce tough fruits. Ground should be well dug but excessive dung causes forking of roots. Plot manured for a previous crop is best suited to turnips.

Successional sowings are done. Seeds are sown in drills 12 inches apart and $^1/_2$ inch deep and later thinned to 6 inches apart. Sowing time is August to December and the crop is ready by October to March.

Improved varieties are *Purple top, Snowball, Golden ball* and *Early milan red top.*

Aphids and saw fly are most likely to attack the turnip crop.

Gardener's Dictionary

Acidic soil	Sour or sharp soil improved with liming.
Alkaline soil	Soil which contains more alkali.
Annuals	Plants living only a year.
Aquatic plants	Water plants
Biennials	Plants completing life-cycle in two years.
Bonemeal	A fertilizer made with decayed animal bones. Chief source of phosphorous.
Brassicas	Plants belonging to cabbage family.
Broadcast	Method of sowing seeds under which seeds are scattred thinly where they are to grow.
Budding	A specialised form of grafting.
Bulb	Globuler stem of some plants.
Compost	Decayed vegetable refuse used as manure.
Deciduous	Subject to periodical shedding.
Dibber	Gardener's implement for planting.
Drill	Small furrow.
Drilling	Sowing in rows.
Fertilizer	Its properties make the soil more fruitful or fertile.

Fruit buds	A cluster of flower-buds which are larger, fatter and rounder than growth-buds.
Growth bud	Producer of a shoot and found in the angle formed by leaf stalk joining the stem.
Heeling-in	During heavy rains or frosty period, when proper planting cannot be done, plants are placed in a slanting trench and roots are covered with soil.
Herbaceous	Herb-like plants.
Hoeing	Loosening ground and removing weeds with hoe.
Hybrid	Offspring of two plants of different species, cross breed.
Inorganic fertilizers	Chemical fertilizers.
Lateral	Any young shoot.
Layering	A shoot fastened down to take root.
Leader	Young shoot required to extend a main branch or a new branch.
Loam	Rich soil of clay, sand and decayed vegetable matter.
Manure	Dung or other substances used for fertilizing soil.
Organic manures	Those substances which owe their origin to plants or animals.
Peat	Vegetable matter decomposed by water and partly carbonized.
Perennials	Plants that survive for many years on coming up year after year.
Plunge bed	Site used solely for sinking pots during summers or for encouraging root growth on freshly potted bulbs.

Propagation — Multiplication or reproduction of plants by sowing, grafting or breeding.

Pruning — Getting rid of dead or over-grown parts, or reducing the luxuriance of plants.

Rind — Bark.

Ringing — Device for checking excessive vigour to encourage fruitfulness.

Scion — Shoot cut for grafting.

Shrub — Woody plant of less size than tree.

Soot — Black powdery substance rising in the smoke of coal and wood and applied as fertilizer.

Spur — A group of fruit buds found on mature fruit trees.

Staking — Stout stick driven into ground to support plants.

Stock — Stump of stem of a tree.

Stopping — Pinching of shoot ends to stop vertical growth of a plant.

Suckers — Shoots springing from plant's roots and not from the stem.

Transplanting — Uprooting and replanting elsewhere.

Trenching — Digging into pits so as to bring subsoil to the top.

Trowel — Flat-bladed tool for lifting small plants.

Tubers — Swellings formed at the root of some plants.